For a SECOND CHANCE, Turn The Page

A STORY OF FAITH, PROPHECY, AND REVELATION

BY

Stacie Bowles

EDITED BY

HANNAH MENSLAGE

Bowles, Stacie. Author
For a Second Chance, Turn the Page

This book is a work of fiction. Any references to historical events, real people, or real places are used fictitiously. Other names, characters, places and events are products of the author's imagination, and any resemblances to actual events or places or persons, living or dead, is entirely coincidental.

Stacie Bowles

In Association with:
Elite Online Publishing
63 East 11400 South #230
Sandy, UT 84070
EliteOnlinePublishing.com

ISBN: 978-1-961801-11-0 (eBook)
ISBN: 978-1-961801-12-7 (Paperback)

FIC042100
REL006140

This book is printed in the United States of America.

TABLE OF CONTENTS

PREFACE

FOR THOSE DISCOVERING THIS topic for the first or you discover a topic you have more questions on, I've crafted a detailed study guide to complement your reading, available for free download. You can easily refer back to this guide as you progress through the book, or you might choose to delve into it later. Access this resource at www.TheRevelationGeneration.com.

Whenever the book touches on content detailed in the study guide, a reference will be made, ensuring you always know where to seek further clarity. For instance, if you come across a mention of the 144,000 witnesses and wonder about their significance, simply consult the study guide. You might also choose to mark that section in your book for future reference.

When I cite biblical passages to support a point, I'll introduce it with, "Let's turn to the word."

CHAPTER 1

IT WOULD NEVER BE THE SAME

IT WAS A BEAUTIFUL summer day; a day to remember. Cassie woke up enthused for her annual trip to Dallas with her three shopping friends. The four, Cassie, Jules, Maddie and Angie, would embark on a road trip to Dallas Market. It was always such an exciting and adventurous trip.

The ladies all worked full-time jobs, but they shared a love for a dazzling gift shop they owned, "Four Southern Chicks," and always eagerly anticipated their yearly trip. At Dallas market, they'd place orders for everything they liked, without their husbands present and complaining about how much they'd spent. But the real fun, historically, was in going back home and waiting for their boxes to show up, one after another.

Opening the shipments, assigning prices for each item, and artfully displaying them in their store always felt like being a child on Christmas morning.

Owning a store was invigorating; being one's own boss had its perks too, but working with friends was a sheer blessing.

Four Southern Chicks was located on the main street in the quaint town of Seeville, a little outside of Houston. It was one of the only local gift shops in the quiet area. It sat in the heart of what once was an old trail station. Central Station was now converted to Hastings Hall, named after the first school teacher in the little town of Seevile.

Hastings Hall still had the original arched windows and tall thick wooden doors. The floors bore scuff marks from the innumerable families who passed through its doors over the years. These stunning wooden floors, still intact, were paired with massive ceiling beams, representative of the strength of the town and the people who built it.

Southern Chicks Gift shop sat in the center. On one side was the local pharmacy which unrelatedly housed the local post office. Yes, Seeville was one of few remaining towns to still have a local pharmacy, a shred of nostalgia from one's grandparents' era.

Directly on the other side of the gift shop was McNair's hardware store with Tiny's barber and shoe shine. Tiny was Dale's son, and tiny he was. Standing just shy of five feet and thin as a rail, he carried an illustrative nickname. This name had a dual meaning; Tiny brought in a select few customers a week, so a tiny space in the back of the store was more than sufficient for his work.

Old man Dale had first dibs after the reconstruction of the train station. No one forgot that it was his grandfather who provided all of the lumber for the original train station. Thus, it was only fitting that he received the first pick to open a hardware store in town. McNair's lumber yard was only a few miles outside of town, but the locals needed a quick place to pick up necessities "in a jiffy," as Dale would often say.

The pharmacist and employees were on a first-name basis with all of the local townies. They were familiar with each person's illnesses and occasional moans and groans. But the best part of Tates Pharmacy was that it still had a soda shop, with drinks from the past, like soda fountain phosphates.

Cassie adored the light, refreshing cherry phosphates. Maddie's drink of choice was the black cow, similar to a root beer float, but with a teaspoon of chocolate syrup. The soda shop also sold a "brown cow," much like the black cow, but with a cola base, rather than root beer, and of course, whipped cream and maraschino cherries on top.

Jules was a creature of habit. She always ordered the orange cream, made with one scoop of orange sherbet, one scoop of vanilla ice cream and orange soda, straight from the bottle. Occasionally, the shop's soda artisan would craft her drink with the orange phosphate drink, which tasted divine.

But Jules preferred her orange cream made with bottled orange soda, most of the time, because the shop worker gave her the half-empty remainder of the bottle. She relished in pouring her soda over the ice cream and sipping the airy foam bubbles that would rise up from the beverage hitting the ice cream.

Angie, on the other hand, was a bit moody. She was frequently indecisive with her orders. In reality, she knew exactly what she wanted, as a woman set in her ways. Yet every time the ladies visited the soda shop, Angie would stand in front of the chalkboard menu, peering at it. Then, she would quietly say, "I think I will try something new."

After a minute or so, Pete, the self-named "Sweet Artesian," would smile fondly at Angie, and ask, "Vanilla malt, no whipped cream?"

"Yes, that sounds good," Angie would respond.

The other three girls still, to this day, do not know if she has ever tried anything new. Perhaps she has once ventured out to a vanilla shake with no malt? Only Pete would know the answer to this one.

They definitely felt like wide-eyed children each time they stepped foot in the soda shop. The ladies would sit at the counter on the high bar stools, people watch and catch up with the gossip of the old timers who would come in. These were splendid times.

Harvey was Cassie's favorite little old man. He only ever entered the pharmacy for essential oils and vitamins. The man didn't take one prescription of any kind. At eighty-eight, the elderly man was stubborn as a mule, but healthy as a horse. It's very possible that Cassie took a liking to him so she could witness to him.

All of the girls were keen on Harvey, but Pete would routinely caution them, "Watch yourself! He is sweet, but if he gets mad at you, he can be as mean as a snake. It's not his mind; no, his mind is sharp as a knife. He's just got a little mean streak in him, and if he isn't getting his way, he will surely snap at you."

Cassie didn't care. She prayed for Harvey regularly, with an adamant determination to not give up witnessing to him. She had feared for his fate ever since she'd heard he didn't believe in Jesus.

He would say, "I am sure there is a creator," and he didn't doubt Jesus existed; he just referred to Him as a good prophet. The locals knew Cassie was beating her head against a wall trying to witness to Harvey, but she wouldn't give up. She relentlessly prayed for him, vowing to do her best to get through to him, even if she had to reach him on his deathbed!

It seemed that the ladies' store, Four Southern Chicks, did so well in this small town because the locals loved the new items they would bring in. Almost every month, the shelves were stocked with new items, but they also consistently carried staples items, like crème brûlée candles, seasonal potpourri, packaged dips and the famous jalapeno raspberry jelly.

At Christmas time, Cassie and her friends were never able to keep jalapeno jelly in stock. At times, they would even keep a cooler on hand, packed with cream cheese and boxes of melba toast, so they could buy all three together. A Christmas party is not complete without jalapeno jelly and cream cheese on melba toast or crackers.

Four Southern Chics proudly sold a variety of unique gifts, like baby items, handmade jewelry from local artists around Texas, floral arrangements and even yard art. The girls ordered as often as possible from local vendors and artists, and they sourced the remainder of their inventory from Dallas Market.

Even at Market, they still aimed to purchase from small businesses, rather than mass-produced imports from giant corporations. The locals in their town of Seeville knew the difference, and they appreciated it.

If you asked a local their favorite aspect of the store, you would hear answers like, "the owners," "the gift wrapping," the shipping service Four Southern Girls offered with their gift wrapping, and free samples of the gourmet food, "try before you buy."

But the most popular feature was the store's homemade fudge. Not that powdered, gas station fudge, in fifty different flavors and colors; real, homemade, "from grandma's recipe" fudge.

Cassie created absolutely decadent fudge. If a townie entered the shop doors at around noon on a Tuesday, they just might be present when she scraped the pot empty and handed out wooden popsicle sticks with a warm sample of a fresh batch of fudge. And if they browsed around the shop a while, they just might be there for the next batch and the next sample.

The delightful cook even took special requests. Last Christmas, one of the town's men asked for pumpkin fudge. This was a tough recipe. It took her several tries to adjust the pumpkin puree with the perfect ratios of cream and vanilla, but she finally perfected it, and it was exquisite.

One day, Jules asked Cassie what she did with the batches that didn't turn out quite right, or didn't harden up.

With a glimmer in her eyes, Cassie responded, "Remember those loaves of pumpkin bread with the glazed icing? The carrot cake with the white chocolate pumpkin icing? The gingerbread cupcakes with the center filling? Each of those were altered recipes with imperfect batches of fudge!"

"And they were so good! We had a fudge tasting contest, and what should have been the top three fudge recipes for last Christmas transformed into six seasonal flavors," Cassie continued with a grin.

"What were the real top three?" Jules asked, puzzled. "The top two had to be that white chocolate maple with walnuts, and the pumpkin fudge. The next four that come to mind are plain chocolate, peanut butter fudge, chocolate pecan and chocolate peppermint."

"Oh, and white chocolate peppermint! That is a total of seven flavors," Jules said.

"Seven is the perfection," Cassie answered, her mouth set in the standard smile she wore before finishing a sentence.

The four women took turns running the shop. It's not that they didn't hire extra help during the year, but they strived to always, and at all times, have one owner present in the store. They'd each work one weekend a month, from Friday to Sunday, and one business week a month, from Monday to Thursday.

This agreement provided each of the girls with a bit of time every month to get away from the hustle and bustle and enjoy peaceful small town living. They shared a charming studio apartment above the store, each occupying the space on the days they worked the shop. There, they enjoyed their precious and infrequent solitude, usually in the evenings, to think and relax.

Cassie dedicated this time to writing her book. Maddie, a socialite, often hung out at the local diner, chatting away all evening with the locals. Angie kept to herself. She was by nature the quiet and introverted type, although when she manned the store, she took on a bubbly persona, making her the highest performing salesperson among the girls.

Maddie cracked jokes about this extreme deviation in Angie's behavior. "She's bipolar!" Maddie would exclaim.

Yet Angie wasn't; she just understood how to turn on her social charm when needed. But at her core, she was a quiet girl. After the store closed every evening, she would flip the "closed til the morning" sign and beeline upstairs to enjoy a peanut butter and jelly sandwich, some chips and her favorite television show.

Cassie, Maddie and Angie were quite perplexed by Jules' post-work habits. In fact, it seemed like the workday, for Jules, never quite ended.

She appeared to be magnetically pulled toward her computer, perpetually answering emails and tending to her full-time job, even when she was working at Four Southern Chicks. Her laptop was permanently opened behind the counter. Out of the four girls, she was the most frequent to try to trade "shop days" with the others.

The ladies had a deal: if somebody picked up one's days without a trade, that person would "bank" the days. At the end of the year, that person would get to take a vacation, and the person who didn't work would have to pay for the vacation, at a rate of a hundred dollars per "banked" day.

And every year, the person funding vacations was Jules. Jules inevitably paid for three vacations per year, because Cassie, Maddie and Angie each all seemed to cover at least one, and often two slots for her.

The three had discussed buying Jules out of her share of the gift shop. It wasn't that Jules didn't care; her full-time work was just so time consuming. However, they'd ultimately decided that the four of them had opened their shop together, in the spirit of sisterhood. It wasn't about money; they were the four chicks behind "Four Southern Chicks," and they couldn't be reduced to three. That just wouldn't work.

The date was June 24, 2022.

Cassie had hardly slept the night before, overly excited for the girls' annual Dallas road trip. She laid awake in silence for hours, missing the muted rhythms of her daughter's rain noise machine from down the hall. Her family was away for the week, and her home felt hollow.

She drifted off to sleep.

Moments later, her morning alarm sounded noisily, stirring Cassie from her slumber.

She glanced briefly at her phone, noticing an unusual number of messages and notifications on the display screen. But she had so much still to do; she had to get dressed and make sure everything was packed for the trip.

"The messages and calls can wait until I'm in the car," Cassie thought. She jumped out of bed, ready to tackle the last of her packing.

But her phone chimed again, with a text from Maddie.

"Turn on the TV," it read. As she scrolled up, she realized that the rest of her unread messages did as well.

Yet Cassie shook her head, dismissing the text.

"I don't watch the news. I'd rather avoid the drama of social media," she thought to herself. She set her phone back down on her nightstand, continuing to prepare for the trip.

Cassie had become slightly sheltered since the days of COVID. This wasn't because she hunkered down; it was quite the opposite, she had followed the rules that were enforced during the lockdowns, but had refused to live in fear, as many others had.

The woman maintained the attitude that if she were infected with COVID, the Lord would heal her, and if it were her time to go, then she knew where she was going. With that tremendous source of security and peace, fear couldn't steal her joy or her life.

Cassie was undeniably a bit different, her views and attitudes setting her apart from others. She often felt as if she lived in her own little world, and she couldn't understand why others didn't think like she did. Her immediate family and her church family were with whom she spent most of her time.

When COVID hit, her attention became hyper fixated on the "end times." She wasn't preoccupied by the same "end of the world" notion as conspiracy theorists, but on a biblical stance. She often stated, confusing many, "I can see the handwriting on the wall."

Cassie's priorities had suddenly and drastically shifted. She had begun to study the Bible and the end times incessantly, and she had devoted the rest of her free time toward writing a book she prayed would save many souls after the rapture. Her book was an instructional guide; what someone should do if they are left behind when the rapture takes place.

Cassie would frequently proclaim that while many are teaching and preaching that Jesus is the Messiah, millions still don't care or don't believe.

"What about those who one day will realize that they were wrong?" She pondered. For if the end days are actually near, and believers are taken up into the sky, the souls left behind can still be saved. But do they even know how?

"It doesn't have to be too late. God is a merciful God, and people need to know that they still have a final chance to accept Christ. But most have no idea what they will face, or how to make it through when the rapture happens," Cassie thought. Fear for and compassion for the unsaved were feelings that swarmed Cassie's mind.

Her friends had mixed emotions. For the most part, they didn't understand what all of the fuss was about. Angie didn't want to hear anything about the "end days." She heard talk of this all of her life, and had ultimately turned from God. Jules didn't have much to say. She would vacantly stare into the abyss when Cassie would discuss prophesized worldly happenings or excitedly share testimonies.

Yet, Jules seemed, on some level, to know something was different in the life Cassie lived. Jules had been present and experienced what some would call miracles that had taken place in the life of Cassie. Jules could not and did not dispute that these were acts of God.

Cassie prayed and believed Jules would wake up one morning and have a hunger for the Lord and never look back. Out of every nonbeliever or non follower of Christ in Cassie's life, Jules puzzled her the most.

She simply couldn't fathom Jules' logic. Why, despite all that the woman had witnessed, did she not desire a close relationship with the Jesus Cassie talked about and the Jesus that was apparently alive and active?

Cassie would say, "Many see Him as a magic wand to wave when you need something, but Jesus is a divine being with whom one should strive toward having a personal relationship with."

Cassie, herself, took great pride in her tight knit connection with her savior. Sometimes even annoying those around her but no one could accuse Cassie of being pushy. It was more of a silent chase.

"Many Christians call on God only when they need Him. Like a parent toward their children, our creator wants us to make time to reach out and bond with Him. Is it that hard to make Him part of your life?" Cassie frequently pondered.

"Does it take too much time out of your day to talk to Him; to learn the power of salvation? Or is there something people are afraid of; a bad experience of sorts? If not, then how could people experience His miracles and still reject a bond with Him?"

These musings wounded Cassie's heart deeply.

Clearing her thoughts with a vigorous headshake, Cassie paused her packing to grab a small remote from her wooden bedside table. She flipped on her television. What were all of these frantic telephone calls about?

Roe vs. Wade is Overturned.

This jarring headline swarmed the dimly lit bedroom in bolded font.

"I knew there was talk about this, but I never thought it would happen," she thought.

Cassie, the early bird, woke up nearly ready to head out. Maddie was quite the opposite. She'd coaxed the girls to meet up and leave later in the day so they could watch the stunning events unfold on the news.

"What a day this will be," Cassie mused, envisioning riding in a car together for five hours post watching the nation's biggest controversy since… she didn't even know when.

George Floyd was a serious incident; Trump being elected, and then impeached nearly every year he was in office was a daily news headline for years. Even now, Russia and Ukraine are at war; gas prices are skyrocketing exponentially; we are experiencing severe food shortages; and heat waves and causing thousands of cattle to die and spontaneous fires to combust.

"Yet the overturn of *Roe vs. Wade*… this was massive. And I have to be cramped in a car with all of them," Cassie thought.

Last year's trip, in 2021, wasn't quite so unique. The year before that was hectic.

Cassie phoned her friend, Belinda, to inquire if she was heading to the market, and more subtly, to find out her take on the new ruling.

"Already on the freeway!" Belinda said excitedly. "I'll be passing by your neck of the woods within the next few minutes. Want to grab a coffee and ride with me? You can meet up with the girls at the market this evening, and get the extra day in!"

"You're right, if I wait for the girls to head out, we won't even make it to the market before it closes for the day," Cassie sighed.

"But I can't bail on them. I would love to meet for coffee, though, and visit for a while."

"Common Grounds Coffee Shop? In fifteen minutes?" Belinda responded.

Cassie grabbed her suitcase, her catalog- and order-storing rolling cart and backpack. She quickly skimmed through her packing list for a final time.

Both phones? *Check*. One was a work phone she used to take notes and listen, almost habitually, to a book on audible or the Bible app.

Phone chargers? Baseball caps (yes, plural)? *Check*.

A pillow, three pillow cases, and her Bo, her teddy bear? *Check*. Why a teddy bear? Just because; it was a comfort thing. Her bear was a bonding experience between herself and her daughter. When they traveled, they teased each other with posed pictures of the bear at coffee shops or cafes with them. The lightly tattered, fading little animal was weathered from their love.

Everyone from Cassie's house was already gone for the day when she left. This made it easier to leave. Cassie loved to travel, but hated to leave home... particularly when her family wasn't going with her. She quickly jotted down a note for everyone, and pinned it to the kitchen bulletin board, and said "Come on Bo, we gotta go!"

She followed that up with a quick text to her family to say she was heading out, and would call when she got there. Then, Cassie was on her way.

The drive to Commons Grounds Coffee Shop was short. Cassie pulled into the parking lot just as Belinda was walking in and shooting Cassie a text to see if she was close by.

"I'm ordering to save time. The usual?" Belinda texted Cassie, as she stepped up to the counter.

Cassie scurried in the large, aging coffee shop doors, threw her backpack on the nearest table, and stepped up to the register just in time to scan her app to pay for their drinks.

"I was getting that!" Belinda laughed fondly, her thin face stretched into a broad smile. She enveloped Cassie in a warm hug.

"Coffee points," Cassie shrugged, covering up her desire to treat her friend. After a short wait, the ladies gripped their coffees and Cassie led Belinda to their table.

As the ladies sat down, Cassie mentioned that she brought her computer to get some work knocked out after Belinda leaves. She'd have a long wait ahead of her, so she might as well do some work, she said.

Belinda wasn't just a friend. She was Cassie's relative and a vendor at the shows that Cassie promoted.

"Are you working on show stuff after I leave?" Belinda asked as Cassie pulled her computer out of her backpack.

"No, I'm working on something else, but I wanted to show you a couple of things. The first is on our website and sort of... behind the scenes," Cassie responded, with an air of mystery.

Tilting her screen toward Belinda, Cassie rapidly pushed a few buttons.

"Here are our Google ratings. We have a marketing firm working on our search engine optimization. We also pursued some new advertising avenues this year, and we were blown away when they showed up where we were ranked! Look at these numbers. We are officially the largest show circuit around, and certainly in a niche unlike any other show," Cassie said excitedly.

"That's amazing!" Belinda breathed incredulously. "I am so impressed. And what is this 'second thing?'"

"Well, I'm working on a book. I actually started it in the summer of 2020, but it feels outdated now, so I'm reworking certain portions and including some of the information in a study guide," Cassie said.

"What's it about?" Belinda asked, the woman's curiosity peaking.

"Oh, I thought I had mentioned it to you. It's an informative book for people who are left behind after the rapture," she responded.

"Or, possibly, it's information to give to an unsaved loved one who may be left behind."

Belinda's eyes illuminated.

"Oh my gosh," she marveled. "At my church, we just started a Bible study course about the book of Revelation. I can't say I have ever heard our pastor preach on this subject. People need to get back to the basics and hear the truth. I really believe that time is running out," Belinda exclaimed.

Without missing a beat, she said, "Honey, hand me some sugar packs."

Tearing open one pack after another and pouring the contents into her coffee, stirring nonstop, Belinda continued.

"I told my uncle, 'Stop, drop and pray today, because stop, drop and roll won't work in Hell.' I have so many family members and friends who won't listen to me. My family is full of heathens," she gaped.

"I don't hold back one lick either! I tell them, 'Plugging your ears won't change the truth. If you die, you fry, because Hell don't have no back door!'"

Cassie was stunned. She tried, with every fiber of restraint in her body, not to succumb to a fit of laughter. Belinda's brows were furrowed in graveness, and Cassie preferred not to offend.

"Belinda!" Cassie scolded. "You can't tell people that!"

"Shoot, I tell my niece all the time, 'You can't shack up with the devil and expect God to pay the rent,'" Belinda doubled down.

"Okay, well maybe you can say that to them, or maybe you just need a box full of my books," Cassie jokes. "But in all seriousness, you need to tell your family, with love, 'We all sin. We all will die. We all will be judged. We can't save ourselves, but Jesus paid the price and paved our way for redemption.'

Belinda's face twisted downward in a slight frown.

"You can't just buy your family a bunch of Bibles, tie a bow around them, and leave a note reading 'Santa is Satan and Christ is Life,'" she countered.

"No, but I'm going to hold a Bible study for you! We need to work on your tactics of witnessing," Cassie said lightly.

The woman felt a hint of anxiety bubbling up her ribcage. She detested arguing with a dear friend, but firmly believed that witnessing must be rooted in kindness and love.

"I met my husband in church, and we've been attending the same church for thirty years. We still sing in the choir. Didn't it take you like twenty years to get Gary in church?" Belinda rebuffed.

"Umm, I married your cousin!" Cassie responded.

The women both burst with laughter, sides heaving, tension diffused.

"So, where was this book conceived?" Belinda asked after their snickering died off.

Cassie leaned toward Belinda, arms folded on the table.

"It kind of started back in 2016. I went to the School of Evangelism with founder Reinhard

Bonnke. Peculiarly, that was the last year that he was hosting the school. While I was there, I was overtaken by a strong sense to witness to the unsaved who might be left behind during the rapture. It felt like a divine calling from God," she said, urgency brimming her tone.

"Interesting," Belinda remarked. "So how did this come about? Why did you attend his school?"

"Well, I applied, and I waited and waited. As time passed, I grew anxious to hear the school's answer. So, I phoned them to find out how long the application screening process took," Cassie said.

"The lady who answered the phone had no idea, but she did reveal that there were over a thousand applicants, each individually sorted through by Reinhard Bonnke. But Reinhard doesn't actually read the applications! He lays his hand on them and lets the Holy Spirit guide his acceptances."

"So I hung up the phone, with the solemn realization that people have applied to this school from all around the world. Only ten percent would be accepted," Cassie continued, recalling her dismay.

"And it felt like ages after that; I can't quite remember the length of time; I finally received my acceptance email. I was peering at my phone in the middle of a grocery aisle, and there it was. I'd gotten in. I broke into a fit of joy, jumping and shouting, which my daughter heard from another aisle," Cassie laughed.

"She popped around the corner, and when she saw the tears of bliss on my face, she knew I'd been accepted."

"And the School of Evangelism, it was a monumental milestone in my life. While I was there, I found my calling. So I began to study, hours on end, gathering and absorbing all I could about end times. What will happen during and after the rapture? How can a person be saved if they're left behind? I needed to know," Cassie said.

She paused to sip her half-emptied coffee. Belinda traced circles on the lid of her cup, pondering her friend's words.

"Say the rapture happens. Will the people left behind still have another chance?" she asked.

Cassie's eyes sparkled with enthusiasm.

"Yes!" she responded. "Redemption and salvation are still possible. God is a merciful God. He doesn't want to see any of His children turn away from Him. If you don't pledge allegiance to the Antichrist by accepting his mark, 'the mark of the beast,' and you accept Christ, you can still make it to Heaven."

At this, Belinda fell quiet in reflection.

"Are there people who know the Lord now and still refuse to accept Him?" the woman asked, apprehensive and fidgeting with her coffee lid.

"Of course," Cassie responded. "Ironically, the people who make the choice to accept and follow Satan as their god know without doubt that Jesus is the Messiah."

"You see, there are those who believe full heartedly that Jesus is the Messiah, and they accept him as their Lord and Savior. There are others whom Satan reaches. I can't explain why; I can't know why; but they choose to serve him. And then, there are those who refuse to make a choice. Fence sitters!" she scoffed.

"This type of person may say, 'I neither believe nor disbelieve, either way.' Or perhaps life has sent them down a path in which they've found themselves mad at God. Or they may have another reason for never accepting Christ. Yet they certainly don't make the conscious choice to accept Satan, either. But if you don't choose Christ, you have, by default, chosen Satan," Cassie explained.

"Wow," Belinda exhaled. "Okay, I need a copy of this book once you've finished it."

Cassie agreed, adding that her friend could also do a rough 'opinion read' on her unedited work. Cassie was curious as to how it would be received.

"Okay, well, tell me about the market last year!" Belinda said, shifting gears. "I didn't make it out."

"Last year wasn't the best. The girls and I stepped foot inside a ghost town!" Cassie exclaimed. "Things did pick up a bit toward the end, but really, I'd chalk it up to COVID."

"The unknown of how long COVID would continue; the stark decline in the economy; the world was a mess! And it definitely affected the market. People were reserved about placing too many orders. Worse than that was what we heard in the first few showrooms."

"See, the limited availability of products and shippings had bred the perfect storm. It was so strange. We were told that there was little inventory. We could place an order, but there were no guarantees of when we'd receive it, or whether or not it would even be in stock! As we spoke with more stores and representatives, chaos continued to reveal. It was like the curtains were pulled back, and we caught a glimpse of how dire the supply chain issues really were," Cassie said incredulously.

Belinda was visibly intrigued, head tilted in deep contemplation.

"Was this a planned phenomenon, as some believe COVID was? You know, I watch TikTok. I keep up with the times, and I know what people are saying!" Belinda professed. "If you want to seek the truth, scour the internet. Nowadays, that's where you go for the nitty gritty information."

"What does your hunch tell you?" Belinda asked rhetorically.

"I mean, look at the domino effect of our economy and the inflation rate since that time frame. It's not just the cost of food, but consider the scarcity of getting chips for cars created a shortage of cars. This paired with supply and demand made car prices skyrocket. Now, the price of everything we purchase has increased severely. And the worker shortage! We see countless businesses begging for employees; many just don't want to go back to work, because they're making more with government supplementation!"

Frustrated, Belinda sighed, "I know many who work side jobs for cash and get checks. Now, all we ever hear about on the news is recession! So, back to my original question, was this all orchestrated? Even if COVID itself wasn't planned, could the economic crisis have been planned?"

"It's funny you say that," Cassie responded. "If we had more time on our hands, I could spew to you an entire sermon over Bible verses which foretell a one world government and a one world monetary system."

"But, with that said, certain steps would be taken to draw our world to that point. What better way to achieve this, than to bring about a financial crash of the global leader?"

"America," Belinda breathed.

"Exactly. America is creeping upon thirty-two trillion dollars in debt. The indications of this are insane. Each citizen, no matter their age, even each baby from birth, owes over ninety-four thousand dollars. Even crazier, each taxpayer owes over two hundred forty-six thousand dollars! These numbers are climbing each day," Cassie said.

"Wow. So, the Bible predicts a one world monetary system and a one world government?" Belida asked, bushy brows raised slightly with concern.

"The Bible doesn't use those exact words. Yet with reading Revelation 13, Daniel 2:41-42 and Daniel 7:8, you can conclude the book predicts this," Cassie responded.

"We're already seeing a wide scale transition to a cashless society. The natural next step would be the one world monetary system. This will set the stage for the 'mark of the beast.' There was a time, merely a few years ago, when anyone who had previously heard of the mark, or chip, from say a grandparent or in church, would simply never accept the mark during the seven year tribulation."

"But now, I think people are so conditioned that it's just the next step. I must say, I never saw this all coming," Cassie mused, almost to herself.

The coffee shop, earlier bustling with conversation, businessmen and hurried morning beverage orders, had died off into a quieter crowd. The two women, heads together and absorbed in their conversation, hardly noticed the scenery shift.

"Remind me. What is the mark?" Belinda asked.

"After the rapture, during the seven year tribulation, the Antichrist will step into power. As a brilliant mind and a smooth talker, he will be revered as the world leader. He will demand that everybody accept this mark, known as 'the mark of the beast' in the Bible. This is what was prophesied, and today, most believe this mark will be a chip," Cassie responded.

"Doesn't the chip already exist? Computerized chips are being used to track children; to enter a workplace; even to purchase food at work! This technology has been integrated into so many domains. It's already here," Belinda fretted.

Cassie soothed. "The key difference is that this chip will come after the rapture. It will be required to buy and sell, and it will be mandated by this leader, the Antichrist. If you were left behind, you could be killed if you don't accept it. But by taking it, you will be accepting this man, and essentially Satan, as your God."

"This is why receiving or rejecting this chip, which will seem like such a small decision during this time, will be the determinant between somebody still being able to accept Jesus Christ, and going to Heaven, or in sealing their future in Hell. We are in a pivotal point in time, where a societal shift, or 'conditioning,' as I call it, is occuring," Cassie continued.

"People of our age demographic, over fifty, and particularly the sixty to eighty year old crowd, won't take fondly to a cashless society. But the younger generation, they rarely use cash now. With the takeover of Cash App, Apple Pay, Venmo and Paypal, and even cryptocurrencies, the cashless society will be second nature to them. Many younger people don't even write checks anymore!" Cassie marveled.

"Actually, I think the post-rapture chip mandations will occur similarly to the public response to the COVID shot," she speculated.

"Keep in mind that this post-rapture world will have completely fallen to chaos, confusion and fear. At first, many will receive the chip, simply due to the ease of buying and selling in the world with a simple mark, just like those who received the vaccine, simply because it was an obvious solution."

"Then, the next stage will be enticements. I expect that people will be incentivized to receive the chip, akin to payments being offered to COVID vaccine recipients. And next, I think they'll ban people without the chip from certain locations and activities, such as traveling and public venues, and possibly public transportation and eating establishments, like with COVID."

"And eventually, people will reach a point in which they must accept the chip in order to buy or sell," Cassie emphasized.

"Oh my gosh," Belinda gasped. "I understand clearly now. We're being conditioned like sheep to slaughter. But how does this relate back to China?"

Cassie smiled at the face across the table. After decades of friendship with Belinda, she was acquainted with her interest in learning. She wasn't surprised that the woman was able to keep pace with the rabbit trails.

Yet she feared the gravity that these conversations would have on her. Awareness of the spiritual destiny of today's world without being consumed in fear is a fragile balance. Certain realizations cannot be unlearned, thoughts occupying the silent moments of one's day.

Shaking her head to clear her mind, Cassie carried on regardless.

"Well, that relates to the Dallas market trip, and the inflation hike within the last couple of years. It's like getting ready for a theater play. Countless preparations are made behind the scenes before the show, and then eventually, the stage is set, and those who present the story walk onto the stage. The audience is wide eyed, awestruck and gullible," she illustrated.

"And in relation to the prices, we see the effects of calculated, behind the scenes efforts as audience members now. But the market served as a peek behind the curtain, and this is what I saw."

"China, the trade superpower of the world, had been shut down for so long that production was halted and inventory was low. Shipping costs skyrocketed from four thousand dollars for one shipping container, coming from China and other countries, to over twenty four thousand dollars for one container. It was the epitome of a supply and demand bidding war."

"One rep put it this way. 'China controls the inventory, and they'll ship it to whomever pays the most,'" Cassie recalled, dumbfounded.

"Right, but it's China!" Belinda exclaimed. "China already has an abundance of products, and the world was shut down for an entire year with purchases tremendously slowed. Shouldn't there be a surplus of supply and plenty of demand? Wouldn't this drive the price down?"

"That's the sad part," Cassie shuddered. "They were charging these prices simply because they could."

"So, last year, we roamed the market, placing orders for what we needed, with set prices of products. We knew the estimated shipping cost. Most showrooms even post market specials, where if you order up to five hundred dollars in product, it's a twenty five percent shipping cost."

"Up to fifteen hundred dollars, for instance, is a twenty percent cap. At three thousand, it's fifteen percent, and at five thousand and over, it's a ten percent cap."

"This tactic persuades shoppers to purchase more from a single showroom, because the company is willing to absorb some of the cost."

"But this time, these companies simply couldn't offer their market specials anymore. The girls and I received emails, and across the board, the wholesalers had eliminated their shipping caps and instituted standard delivery costs based on weight. They even added a surcharge. Within those few months, the products they were selling at market had increased so much in shipping prices that they could no longer honor the prices they offered at market."

Belinda was hunched over, furrowing her brows in concern.

"Yes, so it's going to be interesting to see what's going on with the market this year. Last year, as soon as I realized the gravity of the economic collapse, I would walk in a showroom and the first questions I would ask were, 'Do you have inventory in your warehouse that's ready to ship? What is the expected timeframe of inventory, or are your orders up in the air?'" Cassie responded.

"There were many showrooms at Dallas Market not even taking wholesale orders. They were simply there to greet their customers and maintain their relationships with buyers. I've heard that this year, some companies are reintroducing their printed catalogs from last year, but with new prices reflecting the increase in costs. That's insanity; it took those companies a year to receive their orders! But, I suppose gift items are not the priority to ship out first."

Cassie paused, scooting her seat back as the chair legs screeched lightly across the floor. She stood up.

"We've been here a while now," she said, eyes flickering over the clock on her phone screen. "I'm going to go ahead and grab a sandwich. Would you like another coffee, or something to eat?"

"I am good. Actually, food would make me sleepy. I'm okay with chatting for another forty five minutes or so, and then I'll need to get on the road and head toward Dallas," Belinda responded.

After a few minutes, Cassie returned, right hand clutching a paper bag with a cold turkey and swiss sandwich inside.

"So, I'm curious what the 2020 market was like. Did you get to go that year?" Belinda asked.

"Yes," Cassie answered.

"The girls and I were there that June. This was during the peak of the quarantines, so it was our first adventure outside of our homes, excluding grocery stores, a couple of dinners and a trip to Home Depot. You remember those few months. We were all cooped up for the better part of four months!" she exclaimed.

"That summer, I'd just started putting my notes together to write my book and a few poems flowed as well, here is one that relates to this conversation."

Flipping through her phone, Cassey shared a poem she had written.

"Look how far we've come, yet how we digressed

But who are we really trying to impress?

A disease appeared and our lives were changed,

This time, we as people would never be the same.

Social distancing and standing six feet apart,

Loved ones are dying and families are scarred.

Life was perfect, and just simply convenient.

We live in America; we're protected and resilient.

Who could imagine we'd be in quarantine

Protecting our lives from COVID-19?

Look how far we've come, yet how we've regressed.

But who are we really trying to impress?

How is it we trust Google with any question

But ignore God, Who is pure perfection?

How do we talk to Siri or Alexa everyday

But we can't take a few moments to pray?

We have self-driving cars made by strangers

But can't trust angels that keep us from danger.

You post your lives and hang out on Facebook

When was the last time you had your face in the Book?

Your trust an Uber driver for a ride

But can't pray protection before you drive.

We put more trust in the daily news

Than prophets who wrote what is really the true.

Look how far we've come, yet how we digressed

So now who are we really trying to impress?

I don't want to leave quarantine the same,

Let others point fingers and place the blame.

I know Death is conquered, and we live free

Because Christ died and rose for our victory!"

"That will make you think, I have a question," Belinda interrupted. "It's a bit unrelated, while still related. What if a person does accept this 'mark of the beast,' and they later regret it? Can't they ask for forgiveness and then accept Christ?"

Cassie shook her head slowly, a sad frown creeping onto her face. Mind toying between different explanations, she searched for the best. She took a slow, deep breath, looked down, and simply said "Nope!"

"No," she reiterated. "Jesus shed his blood for your forgiveness and salvation, and for the church to accept Him. He offers grace, mercy and forgiveness now, but after the church has left the earth, you cannot both take the mark and serve the Antichrist, and serve Christ."

"Besides, if you know better, and you missed the rapture, why in the world would you risk it?" Cassie anguished. "You're playing Russian roulette with God!"

"There's a verse you should make a note to go and read, 2 Thessalonians 2:7. '*For the mystery of lawlessness is already at work; Only he who now restrains it will do so until he is out of the way,*'" she quoted.

"This means only the Holy Spirit holds the power to keep sin from boiling out of control. This world has already fallen, and sin has been intensifying over the years. When the church is removed from the earth, people will desperately need the earthly influence of the Holy Spirit, who dwells within the body of the church. Lawlessness will rise faster than our national debt. Simply put, no, you can't take the mark and then ask for forgiveness," Cassie huffed, frustrated with the state of the world and the pace of downfall's escalation.

Belinda nodded; her curiosities were satisfied by her friend's answer.

"Okay, you can tell me more about your previous trip to the market," Belinda said.

"Well, I wrote about it in my book. I'll just read you the first chapter, so I don't skip over any details of that trip," Cassie said, opening her laptop once more.

After pressing a few keys, she began speaking.

"When the Revelation Generation book took on its first words, officially or unofficially, all of America had been following the 'stay at home' ordinance that began mid-March of 2020," Cassie began.

"In retrospect, we'd heard about COVID hitting China that February at a higher rate than most diseases we were familiar with in the past. Viral videos circulated, reporting death tolls which were astronomically higher compared to the numbers reported by the Chinese government. Yet in America, we felt safe and secure, confident we'd remain untouched by the illness."

"Then, the first in-country case appeared in Washington state on January 21. The virus swiftly swept the nation, and by March 4, a case was reported in our own backyard, Fort Bend County, followed by a death. COVID officially commanded our attention," she mused.

"The nation was glued to the television, watching case numbers. Ten people were sick; ten turned to twenty; twenty grew to forty; eighty. By mid-March, a slight sense of fear crept the land. We noticed the numbers were doubling daily. Most became cautious in public, yet we believed this would soon pass."

"This sense of security was quickly crushed."

"Out of the blue, one week after Houston saw its first COVID case, the Houston rodeo was canceled. The 'stay at home' order was issued, and overnight, our lives flipped upside down. This was only the beginning of something we might have labeled a 'conspiracy theory' just months earlier."

"But conspiracy theory or not, these events will be recorded in history books," Cassie read, glancing up from her glowing screen to catch Belinda's eyes, wide and agape.

She continued explaining to Belinda her previous trip to Dallas Market, as well as the global conditions that urged her to write her book.

Reflecting upon the summer of 2020 astonished Cassie, though she'd lived through it firsthand. As those months raced through her mind, she recalled believing COVID would soon be a thing of the past. She thought that it would vanish as quickly as it spawned, leaving a trail of devastation in its shadow.

Cassie laughed, recalling a conversation with an event coordinator at the convention center. She'd asked him if they could just wait a few weeks to see if it would pass.

"No," the man had said, "We are calling it."

And just like that, the second spring market was canceled.

Cassie quickly finished reading what she'd written, packed up her belongings, bid her friend farewell, and headed out the door.

Outside the cafe, Cassie shot Angie, Maddie and Jules quick texts to ensure they were on their way out. Then, she started the engine and sped over to their meeting point. Flipping on her favorite Christian radio station, Cassie enjoyed a few songs in her final moments of solitude. There was nothing quite like worship tunes to shift her mood toward peace.

Recognizing she'd arrive a few minutes early, she made a quick right to pull through a drive-through. The best breakfast a girl could have was a large sweet tea and a chicken biscuit.

The person who designed the T-shirt that reads "raised on sweet tea and Jesus" must have had Cassie in mind, she mused to herself. She was a country girl at heart, unafraid of speaking her mind, and her mind listened to her heart every time.

Moments later, Cassie pulled up and parked next to Jules. She grabbed her suitcase, backpack and food. While walking up to the woman's Suburban, she spotted Maddie and Angie driving up.

Jules popped the hatchback and Cassie chunked her suitcase in, yelled "Shotgun!" and jumped in the front seat.

Angie crawled in next, stowing her one backpack between the seats.

"Excuse me! Can anyone help me with my bags?" Maddie shouted.

Cassie, accommodating by nature, hopped out of her seat and helped her friend stuff her suitcase, backpack and duffel bag full of crafting supplies in the car.

"We're going to Dallas Market, not a camping trip," Cassie emphasized, laughing at her friend's ridiculous overpacking. "We're only going to be gone for three nights!"

"Yeah, yeah," Maddie rolled her eyes. "I need to get my purse!"

Maddie proceeded to paw the most oversized purse Cassie had ever seen, along with a hand towel, a pillow, a coffee and her infamous Yeti cup. The girls didn't dare to ask what was inside of it.

"Is everyone set? Coffee, purse and earplugs?" Jules piped from the driver seat.

Finally, the girls hit the road.

Aside from their quaint gift shop, Four Southern Chicks, each of the four worked other full time positions.

Cassie was a promoter, Jules worked in real estate, Maddie was a doctor and Angie was a school teacher. They all shared different backgrounds in retail and marketing, and formed a cute and lively group. In business, their energies meshed beautifully, but as friends, they clashed in many areas. Politics and religion were their most blatant incompatibilities.

Cassie and Angie were polar opposite personalities. The group dubbed Cassie the "Jesus freak," constantly in church, reading her Bible daily and listening solely to Christian music. They ogled when Cassie spoke of Jesus and of "going *home* soon."

To the other girls, it seemed as if Cassie's days revolved completely around God. Yet if you asked Cassie, she'd simply state that she loves God, recognizes Jesus as the Messiah and walks and talks with the Holy Spirit daily.

Cassie didn't find her behaviors unusual at all; she found integrating God into her daily life as natural as eating and breathing.

Angie, on the other hand, Cassie found quite unusual. Angie called herself an atheist and refused to hear about Jesus or Heaven. She regularly professed Christians as crazy fanatics who try to "brainwash people" into adopting their beliefs. Yet Angie wasn't always this way.

Cassie yearned to talk with her and reason with her, but after multiple shut down attempts, she sensed that Angie's heart would have to be changed by God. She knew that the best approach she could take was being a light and being a friend.

Angie was raised in a Christian family, without a single family member being stranger to the Lord. But the woman had experienced a childhood full of abuse and trauma. She'd endured events that imprisoned her in hurt and in an inability to forgive.

Her father left her family when she was two years old. He committed to three more marriages, and didn't find happiness in any of them. His last marriage destroyed him physically, mentally and financially. This relationship robbed Angie and her sister of their father. He became a shell of a person with no emotional presence and very little physical presence in their lives.

Now, Angie lived only a few minutes away from her father, yet he chose his new family and children over her. This heart wound festered in the woman, who had no idea how to dress her pain. It ate at her. She just couldn't understand why he'd abandoned them. How could she trust a Heavenly Father when her physical father didn't want her.

Yet, the straw that broke the camel's back was her mother's death. She passed away prematurely, only fifty one years of age, from liver cancer. Angie was shattered. She became consumed with fears for her small daughter, not only an absent grandfather, but she would now never know her grandmother.

Almost ten years later, Angie lost one of her grandmothers that had come to live with her due to Dementia. That may seem natural, but in the same week, her other grandmother passed. How often does one have two loved ones graduate from this world within a week.

In long ago conversations about her losses with Cassie, infrequent as they were, Angie had referred to herself as ET.

"I feel like I was left behind," Angie had confided in her friend, tears brimming her eyes. "Remember that movie? ET pointed to the sky and said, 'ET go home.' That is how I feel."

At some point, Angie abandoned her desire to "go home." She'd lost her belief in a home to return to. Lonely and hurting, she bitterly rejected all conversation about God.

And a few years later, her hard heart marbleized. Angie was standing in a crowded auditorium, scanning the sea of faces in pursuit of her step father, Burt. He was nowhere to be found. Angie took her seat and watched her daughter walk the stage of her high school graduation.

The next morning, the now middle-aged mother received a call that Burt had fallen ill. Angie and her family filed into their car and drove twelve hours, arriving just in time to speak their goodbyes. Then, Angie's sister pulled Burt off life support. His hernia surgery had been botched, and just like that, he was gone. One more family member vanished into the ethers.

These tragedies were among many events that steered Angie toward anger at God. Yet despite the devastations in her friend's path, Cassie couldn't fathom this anger. She had her own hurts and devastations but the anger fell to men, not to God.

"Why do people really blame God?" she'd often muse. "He created us because He wanted a family. He loved us so much that He sent His Son to shed His blood and die on the cross as a sacrifice for us. This forged a straight path for us to get back home to Heaven."

Cassie could continue this tangent for a while. It gravely saddened her that her dear friend, along with countless others, had simply stopped believing.

"God is not to blame. He loved us more than life itself, because we are His life," she thought.

Maddie was quite a different story.

She'd grown up in church and wholeheartedly believed in God. While she didn't adamantly believe so, she entertained the idea that Jesus could be the Messiah. However, as an adult, she'd decided that she'd had enough of "talk about hellfire and brimstone."

Jules was a complex character. She'd entertained both disbelief and belief in God at various points in her life, and had neither strong church nor Christian acquaintance backgrounds to influence her.

In childhood, Jules wasn't taught a strong stance either way. She hadn't accepted Christ but did believe in His existence.

For many years, Jules was largely ambivalent and fence-sitting. Yet through a few profound, inexplicable life experiences, she'd begun to believe that there might be something more to "this 'Jesus' story."

Evidence couldn't be disputed; Cassie believed that Jules had already seen enough proof of the higher power in the years they'd known each other. She couldn't comprehend Jules' disinterest in pursuing a closer, living relationship with Jesus. However, she wouldn't force her own views onto Jules. Instead, she offered friendship, silently anxious to answer or explain any question that she might have.

Jules was among the two friends who occupied Cassie's heart. The other was John, her Jewish friend. Both had witnessed Cassie endure more unusual events than most would hear about within a lifetime. Cassie had believed these happenings would steer them closer to God, but they both continuously seemed disinterested in knowing the source of the many miracles.

John and Jules were similar, yet opposite. Jules did believe in Jesus, but Cassie yearned for her to know so much more. She wanted her friend to walk with Him, to feel His presence, to see Him active in her life and to have an insatiable hunger to know Him more.

"How do you do what you do?" Jules would frequently ask Cassie.

"When you are ready, sit down and I will explain the power of God in my life. I'm nothing special; I'm guided by Him. I have faith in Him, and I go to my Father on a daily basis, not just when I need Him to do something for me," Cassie would respond.

As a parent, how would you feel if your child never spoke to you, hugged you or asked how you were doing? How would it affect you if they only spoke to you when they needed help, money or a ride somewhere? It would hurt. Cassie pondered regularly about those who didn't understand how this relationship felt.

Cassie didn't carry the same emotional burden for Angie that she held for Jules and John. Angie had known God as her savior from childhood; she knew that Jesus is the Messiah. Cassie knew Angie's decision to turn her back on God was conscious. She'd become hard hearted.

Back in the car, everybody was set and ready for the trip.

"Now, we head west," Jules declared as she fastened her seatbelt, flipped the radio on, and reversed out of the parking lot.

Once the girls were on the road, Cassie smiled to herself. A weekend of shopping with the girls, this was going to be awesome.

A bellow from the backseat interrupted Cassie midthought.

"So, I see you didn't watch the news this weekend, but you had time to go and spend your money on a chicken biscuit!" Maddie hollered.

"Yep, I heard the news, but I agree with the CEO," Cassie retorted. "Looks like you're drinking the Kool-Aid by spending your money at that coffee shop!"

Maddie religiously kept tabs on the latest business drama. She was quick to tell the girls how they spend their money reflects who they support and their morals.

"Did I miss something this weekend?" Jules asked inquisitively.

The girls turned toward a quiet voice in the back.

"Guys, no politics and no religion, or we won't make it on this long drive!" Angie scolded with a laugh. "Better yet, I'll get out now and Uber home."

The woman looked at Jules.

"It's just another hot button item stemming from the Black Lives Matter protest. It seems like it started off as a political conflict, but now, even the Christians are debating among themselves. You would think they'd all just keep their mouths shut, like we need to do to enjoy our trip!" Angie exclaimed.

Jules chuckled.

"The sad reality is that since quarantine, there hasn't been much to talk about. Life has slowed to a crawl. The biggest speaking points for the last three months have been 'What restaurant will you eat at when we can venture out in public again?' Come to think of it, has anyone gone out to a restaurant yet?" she asked.

"I've been out a couple of times!" Maddie piped.

"I love going to restaurants that have big, open-concept patios. I've learned that I can enjoy dining out, but not dining in around other people. But the first time we went out to eat after quarantine was completely different than what I'd anticipated," Cassie chimed in eagerly.

"I remember when they first announced restaurants would reopen with limited seating," Cassie continued. "I was so excited; we might as well have been going to Hawaii! I called one of my favorite restaurants, one that we enjoy going to after church. It was open, so we went, but it was an odd feeling."

Cassie shuddered, vividly recalling how drastically the world had changed. Even ordinary moments, like dining out with her family, would never be the same, at least for the next year.

"There was one other table, in the entire restaurant," Cassie enunciated, "that a couple was seated at! They left a few minutes after we walked in, so we cracked jokes about reserving the restaurant just for us to be alone. The tables on either side were covered with 'reserved' signs, so that each table occupied would be six feet apart."

"Our server handed us a paper menu with limited entrées, which was understandable considering the circumstances. But no music was playing! The silence made the atmosphere that much eerier, so we played music from my phone and giggled about making the best of an odd situation. What about you, Jules and Angie? Have either of you two gone out to eat yet?"

"Just take out. We've been doing a lot of take out," Jules responded.

"Nope, we're just not ready to go out and eat. I worry about whether or not the employees are wearing a mask, or coming in to work sick! I've heard countless horror stories about that," Angie said.

"I know we said no politics or religion, but I have a couple of questions I'm hoping Cassie can answer," Jules said, quickly shifting the conversation back to the forbidden topics.

"Have at it," she stated blankly. "I'm tired. I stayed up late watching a movie, so I'll take this time to sleep."

Angie audibly rolled her eyes.

With that, Angie reached in her bag and pulled out her headphones. She turned on a song, tucked her knees into her chest, and leaned her head against the window for a cat nap, obviously avoiding the conversation that would unfold.

Ignoring Angie's pouting, Jules took a brief glance in the rearview mirror, and then she turned her attention toward Cassie. She began to describe, in scattered detail, various occurings over the past few months.

"It just doesn't make sense! Too many shocking events have conspired to be considered sheer randomness. I think we're puppets, and our world is being controlled in the background," she proclaimed.

"Well, give me an example. What in particular are you seeing that you're questioning?" Cassie asked.

Jules snorted. "Firstly, this COVID thing just doesn't add up!" she breathed.

"We've had countless previous pandemics. We know how many people die, annually, from the flu. I understand that people fear the unknown, and I understand that COVID has had a higher death toll than the flu, but it still does not add up!"

"I've heard people talking about a vaccine containing a 'chip' of sorts so they can track us. I've heard other people speaking about a 'cashless society,' why is this so significant? We already use our phones, apps and credit cards more frequently than cash, so why is there fear of a cashless society?" Jules continued.

"Killer hornets were the focal point of the media up until recently. I swore that this would be the next big pandemic, but they seemed to disappear when George Floyd was killed. Where did the killer hornets go? And now, with all of this rioting and looting and people fighting!" Jules gasped.

"This is not the America I grew up in. Oh, and there's something else that bothers me. What is this 'contact tracing' with COVID exposure notifications?"

"All of that is a conspiracy theory. You're drinking the Kool-Aid," Maddie chastised Jules.

Angie, who was apparently feigning her sleep, shifted up in her seat.

"Next, y'all will start talking 'rapture theory.' If you're not careful, aliens will come to abduct every last one of you crazy Christians!" Angie chuckled mockingly from the backseat, breaking her brief stretch of silence.

Cassie sighed.

"You're both right, but sadly, you're both wrong," she said. She jerked her head around, peering intensely at the women in the backseat.

"Maddie, you're educated enough to realize that the rapture is coming. Angie, if you believe the saved would be taken by aliens, rather than God, you're drinking the Kool-Aid. But the reality is, you're both living a lie by denying any of this will happen."

"This might be a good time to tell you all about my book, since I'm planning on giving y'all the first copy," Cassie continued.

The car flooded with high pitched inquiries from her three friends, who were shocked Cassie had been sneakily writing a book, and curious about the contents.

"Well, I feel like you all know that I feel in my heart the Lord has given me a calling," she started.

"I know that I've been given the task of witnessing to people who will be left behind when the rapture takes place. It's not that I wish to be left behind; the end days will be horrifying. All Christian churches preach that those who accept Christ will be taken up to Heaven, but very few preachers actually educate about the end times, much less what to do if you are left behind."

"This means that those who will be left behind do not have the information they need to be saved. And what about the Christians with unsaved family members and friends? Wouldn't they want to provide their loved ones with information about what to do, if they're left behind?" Cassie asked pointedly.

She looked directly at Jules.

"All of the questions you just asked, I can explain, and in great detail."

Angie snickered sarcastically, her face snide. She was fed up with Cassie's teachings, a fact not unknown to Cassie.

"You're wasting your time, but it might be a great novel," Angie gibed.

"If I'm wrong, I'm wasting my time, but if you're wrong, you've wasted your eternity," Cassie calmly responded, boldly and without a hint of malice in her tone.

As exasperated as her friend was, Cassie cared deeply for her fate, knowing that these decisions were ultimately Angie's. She silently prayed, asking God for the power to reach her friend's hardened heart, and the hearts of the other women in the car.

"I have heard all of my life, 'The rapture is coming! Jesus is returning! Get your life right!' I'm almost sixty years old, and I'm still hearing this!" Angie exhaled.

Jules, who had remained silent during the past few minutes, eyes trained on the road, spoke up.

"Angie, you're delusional. Maddie, you're in denial. Maybe I'm just uninformed. I think I want an explanation for what's going on, and then I will come to my own conclusion, without the input from you two," Jules said, gesturing behind her head toward the women in the backseat.

"If Cassie can't convince me, then so be it. But give me the facts, and let me use my own discernment, if that's fair," she firmly stated.

Briefly closing her eyes, Cassie thanked God for answering her prayer. She now had an opening to touch the journey of one of the people she held dearest.

Moments like these gave Cassie life. Somebody she cared for would actually listen to her testimonies with a clear mind and heart. "Fake religion" had confused so many other people that she knew. Christians notoriously sat back and bickered amongst themselves, a phenomenon deeply disturbing to Cassie. No wonder the world considered believers crazy!

But now, Cassie had the chance to open her Bible and provide Jules with proof; not just of things that will come to pass in the future, but of tangible, recorded events going on in the world today.

Her mind flashed to the verse in the Bible where all will stand before God one day, and hear or not hear, "Well done, my good and faithful servant."

And Cassie now had a moment in time to not only witness to someone open minded and looking for an answer, but to speak with someone asking for the hard core facts, proof and evidence. She felt as if she was sharing a car with her judge and jury in the backseat, and this was a case she must win.

"Okay Jules, as I said, I can answer all of your questions, but I need to open the Bible and take the time to cross-reference and show you what I'm going to tell you," Cassie started.

"When I have an explanation that is too elaborate for a conversation here, I will write out more information for you to review later on. I will make notes along the way, jotting down your questions and numbering them. Actually, I think I will put those into a study guide for my book for others to read!" she exclaimed.

"Yes, I think I will do that, and I will title it, 'Let's go to study this in depth.'"

"This is going to be so cool. This could get to be too much information to include in my book, but if a reader really wants to dive deeper, this portion will serve as a study guide. Better yet, I will print one book without it and add them to my website and then do another printing with the study guide. Thanks, Jules!" Cassie voiced rapidly, intrigued with this new idea.

Jules laughed sharply.

"Glad I could help, do I get an honorable recognition?" she interjected.

An onlooking pedestrian might glance upon the vehicle, a suburban rolling down country roads, and never give it a second thought. But the inside of the car told a separate story.

In the front seat sat two women, eagerly engaged in an energetic conversation. In the back seat sat a silent and stoic two, one close minded and the other close eared. The atmosphere was direly divided.

"While we're driving, I can still give you an outline about events that will come to pass. But then, we must sit down, because I need to show you, in writing, the evidence. Let's start with some background information," Cassie continued.

"When you have questions, I will provide you with information from the Bible. We'll call this 'Let's go to the Word.' I'll keep this short and simple, but I'll back up what I'm saying."

"Give her the Reader's Digest version," Maddie piped up.

Cassie inhaled deeply, allowing her lungs to expand fully before exhaling. Then, she began.

"For two thousand years, the Gospel has been preached that Jesus Christ is the Messiah. Many believe; many do not. Some say, 'I have been hearing this all of my life.' We go about our lives, executing our day to day activities and planning our futures, yet something massive is on our horizon," she said.

"It's the summer of 2020, and we live in one of the largest cities in America. So many unforeseeable factors are at play all around us; so many unbelievable events. The tension and volatility in the atmosphere have led almost all Christians toward the same belief: we must be nearing His return."

"Many are having dreams of the rapture without realizing it, until they share them with those who understand. Many say, 'I have heard of His return, and I am tired of hearing about it.' And I get it," Cassie proclaimed.

"The second coming of the Lord and the rapture have been preached about since Jesus Christ himself first spoke of this with his disciples when He ascended into Heaven."

Let's go to the Word: 2 Peter 3:3 *"First of all, you must understand that in the last days' scoffers will come, scoffing and following their evil desires. They will say, 'Where is the 'coming' he promised?'"*

Cassie glanced over at Jules. The woman's eyes were still fixed on the road, but her grip on the steering wheel tightened, with that one thumb tapping the steering wheel to the tune of the gears turning in her mind.

"Actually, I remember my grandparents making comments like, 'Now, the Lord can return.' I'd also catch them in these urgent, hushed conversations with each other about Israel becoming a state. They wouldn't elaborate about either topic. How do these relate?" Jules asked.

"Great question, Jules," Cassie affirmed with a slight nod.

"This was the talk of the town back in 1948. When Israel became a nation, even the sinners understood and started going to church. See, Israel becoming a nation and returning to their land was one of the great prophecies to unfold. That year, everyone was saying 'He's coming soon,' but there were still things that had to occur to fulfill the end time prophecies."

"Do you remember hearing about Trump declaring Jerusalem the capital of Israel, and moving the embassy there? This could be considered the last prophecy that needed to happen. The bottom line is, yes, many have been hearing about 'the end' all of their lives. But never before have so many prophesied events taken place as they have in recent years," Cassie declared.

"Never before has so much taken place and been exposed as the world has witnessed within the past few months. Now, all of the sudden, you'll hear chatter everywhere you turn. Even people who are unfamiliar with the rapture can sense that something is brewing."

"And for many, COVID was the final straw. People's eyes have opened. This could be due to the talk of the 'chip,' the government financially supporting an entire country, contact tracing or countless other ominous developments."

"I mean, why do we have a coin shortage, when we've all been at home and not spending cash in public? Why do we wear a mask walking into a restaurant, but take it off when we sit down at our table? How does it make sense that we can attend church, but we're not allowed to sing? Can anybody explain these things?" Maddie emphasized, illustrating with hands as she spoke.

CHAPTER 2

THE SPIRITUAL BATTLE IS BREWING

JULES GLANCED AT CASSIE.

"I vaguely recall hearing something about Israel and the embassy. I suppose I just don't pay enough attention to the affairs of other countries. I figured those were their political issues," she admitted.

"Jules!" Maddie gasped. "Every country surrounding Israel has threatened to blow them off the face of the map. They're still here due to God's protection, just as he protected them during the six-day war. My parents have been using the expression 'when there is peace in the Middle East' my entire life!"

"I have never heard of peace in the Middle East. It seems the conflict there is endless," Jules marveled.

Cassie grunted in agreement.

"Exactly. They have been fighting since the days of two brothers named Isaac and Ishmael," she responded.

"Who are they?" Jules asked.

"Abraham was promised by God to be the father of all nations," Cassie began. "He was old and still without children. His wife Sarah said, 'I am too old, you need to go in with our servant Hagar and bear a child.' And Abraham did so, disobeying God's timing, and birthed a child with Hagar. This was Ishmael."

"Abraham was eighty-six years old at the birth of Ishmael. Fourteen years later, when Abraham was one hundred and Sarah was ninety, they birthed their son Isaac. Some years later, Sarah told Abraham that it was time to send Hagar and Ishmael away."

"This began the longest family quarrel in history. In fact, it has lasted four thousand years. Muslims believe that because Ishmael was firstborn to Abraham, they are entitled to Israel. Christians and Jews believe that Isaac was the promised son through the bloodline of Abraham and Sarah, and therefore, they're entitled to the land promised to Abraham by God."

"See, it was specified in the bible that God would give this land to Abraham's children and dependents," Cassie explained.

Silence echoed in the car for a few minutes as Jules contemplated Cassie's words. In the backseat, Maddie looked thoughtful, and Angie glared out the window.

"So, how does this relate to the incessant fighting in the Middle East, the embassy and the capital?" Jules asked, puzzled.

Cassie briefly explained to her friend the relationship between these elements.

"Jewish people were without their land for all of these years. Israel was historically ruled by other countries and leaders, and the Jewish people have been in and out of bondage for most of their existence," she stressed.

"Like the Holocaust," Jules breathed.

"Precisely," Cassie concurred. "Their entire existence has been threatened by countries and people who wish to obliterate them; to erase them. From their bondage in Egypt to the Holocaust, you can point to multitudes of periods during which nations sought to enslave these people. So, why are they so hated?"

Maddie again broke her quiet, eagerly leaning forward on the car console.

"Because the Jewish are God's chosen people!" she boomed. "Satan hates them, and he has used his silver tongue to convince the world to hate them."

"That was blunt," Cassie laughed humorlessly. "Yet accurate. Just as Satan tried to halt the plans of God through Jesus Christ, he has ceaselessly targeted the race of the Jewish people. Then, there's the significance of the capital and the embassy. These aren't merely battles over land, nor over the declaration of Jerusalem becoming the official capital."

"It's the prophecy being fulfilled! Satan is aware of what was written two and even four thousand years ago. He isn't blind to the ultimate outcome; he resided in Heaven before he was thrown out. If the world were a baseball game, we'd be in the ninth inning, with Satan losing desperately and zero chance of overtime."

A voice sounded from the backseat, causing every girl's head to whip around in curiosity.

"What exactly does this have to do with the coronavirus? With the impeachment of and hatred for President Trump? I'll admit that I find it somewhat interesting," Angie said, swallowing, "The timing of the embassy, and all of the fighting. And yes, I've seen the news, I'm aware of what happened after the declaration was made."

"So, continue, Cassie. Let's hear all about this spiritual battle that is brewing." Angie said begrudgingly, jutting her chin slightly to save face.

Cassie smiled to herself, well aware that Angie's snarky tone was a ploy. As much as Angie struggled to admit it, she was intrigued. She was open. Maybe not reachable. This tickled Cassie's heart tremendously.

"The world is in the deep throes of a spiritual battle like never before," Cassie began, holding Angie's gaze. "I've met some who believe that murky, dark cloaked deals were made to get President Trump out of office because they couldn't find substantial evidence to impeach him. But my question is, why was this one man hated so vehemently? Impeachment talks began the moment he was elected!"

"Why not just wait until the next election cycle, and run a stronger candidate against him so that he isn't reelected? Let's abandon all personal feelings toward Trump for a moment. Wouldn't you agree that our government and media have taken extreme measures to throw him out of office, rather than letting his presidency run its course and then electing somebody new? The root of this isn't a political battle; it's a spiritual battle."

"The Bible says the enemy has but a short time, and will do everything in his power to bring destruction and chaos in the last days. We've never before witnessed such drastic polarization among people in so many facets of life. People are divided politically, racially and spiritually, and that disparity keeps widening. The hostility keeps growing."

"In the past, you'd have your views, others would have theirs, and you'd still get along. Lately, if you have a minority opinion, your family, friends and coworkers will turn against you. The gospel has been preached, and of course, many reject it. This is their free will. But when the Antichrist seizes power, people will be forced to serve one religion, and killed if they refuse."

"Many have dedicated their lives to testifying to others and reaching lost souls. Yet the more I look around, the more people I encounter who have rejected it. My heart urges me to reach those I can, to educate people about the path to being saved after the rapture. Even if they dismiss Christ as the Messiah now, they still have a chance, and they must know this."

"And what do you think will happen when the rapture commences?" Cassie posed with a wry laugh.

"Millions will disappear in the blink of an eye. You may or may not realize that only Christians vanished. You must decide at this point if we were preaching the truth. Or, perhaps it was an alien invasion. I promise, this is what you will be told."

"Society strategically teaches the misnomer 'The wicked will be removed from the earth.' When the Christians are raptured, this is what you'll hear. Christians will be labeled 'the wicked' because they followed the rules of God. Although not every 'Christian' follows the teachings," Cassie remarked, wiggling her fingers in makeshift quotation marks.

"And after the rapture, plenty of pseudo-Christians will remain. Meaning, many people today call themselves Christians and are not. There is a verse in the Bible, Revelation 2:9 and Revelation 3:9 that references, *'not all who call themselves Jew are truly Jew.'*"

Jules nodded slowly, absorbing Cassie's words.

"Is that what the book is about?" she asked.

"Yes," Cassie agreed. "I'm hoping my book serves two purposes. The first is to offer salvation instructions to people left behind. Secondly, I want to include enough evidence in my book that I can reach people before the rapture even transpires."

Cassie glanced at her friends in the car, quickly assessing their body language. Maddie was leaning forward in the backseat, face tensed in concern and intrigue. Jules, driving, watched the road almost absently, thoughts visibly circling her mind.

Even Angie seemed more receptive, head turned a miniscule degree toward Cassie, though still faking disinterest.

"What specifically is the rapture? If we're left behind, how is it possible that we have another chance?" Jules questioned.

Maddie grunted in agreement.

"Yes, explain the 'rapture,' Cassie. I have scoured the Bible, and I've seen nothing about this," Maddie declared with an air of confidence.

Cassie smiled.

"Well, let's go to the Bible," she said. "You're absolutely right, Maddie, in that the word 'rapture' is nowhere in the Bible. For that reason, many reject the teaching altogether."

"'Rapture' is a common term used for 'catching away.' The word 'rapture' may not be in the Bible, but neither are terms like 'demon,' Catholicism and trinity. The word 'bible' isn't even in the Bible, and yet we use them in our language," she explained.

Let's go to the Word: Here is why we use the English word rapture. The Greek Word harpazō means "to seize," or "to snatch out/away" from harm's way. 2 Corinthians 12:2 reads "*I knew a man in Christ above fourteen years ago, (whether in the body, I cannot tell; or whether out of the body, I cannot tell: God knoweth;) such a one caught up to the third heaven."* And in Revelation 12:5 declares *"And she brought forth a man child, who was to rule all nations with a rod of iron: and her child was caught up unto God, and to his throne."*

Angie stirred from the backseat.

"So what's next, Cassie? Are you going to write another book to prove who Jesus is?" she smirked.

Cassie issued a single, droll laugh.

"No," she shook her head. "Quite the opposite. When the rapture takes place, I won't need to prove anything. God Himself will have spoken. 'A picture is worth a thousand words,' they say, but the picture of earth at that time will render you speechless."

"Yet the purpose of this book isn't confrontation," she mused. "I'm not writing to debate, argue or assert personal opinions or claims. I will provide verses as evidence, but it's up to readers to study the Word and reach their own conclusions. I am aiming to spread information that could potentially help the left behind save their souls," Cassie continued.

"Remember my words, Angie. If I am wrong, I have wasted my time. If you are wrong, you will waste your eternity. If in reading my book, somebody finds that they are not living the life they should, or have not accepted Christ as their savior, I pray that they will accept Christ."

Cassie flipped through the pages of the weathered leather Bible resting on her lap. She paused on one, pointer finger gliding across the heavily annotated paper.

"John 3:18 reads, *'He that believeth on him is not condemned: but he that believeth not is condemned already because he hath not believed in the name of the only begotten Son of God,'*" Cassie quoted.

Beside Cassie, Jules muttered something indecipherable to herself. Cassie turned toward her, interest piqued.

"Can we discuss this deeper?" Jules asked, voice now clear. "I suppose I need to learn some basics. It feels like I'm trying to put a puzzle together without the box top for reference."

Cassie nodded, equally eager to elaborate.

"Absolutely!" she chirped. "This would be a great time to acquaint you with the study guide that is available on the website TheRevelationGeneration.com."

CHAPTER 3

YOUR SOUL IS AT STAKE

"WOW," JULES BREATHED. "THIS is a lot of information. Let me make sure I'm following all of this. Jesus snatches His followers from earth at an unknown time, returns them home to Heaven, and then still provides those remaining a last chance to accept Him?"

"Yes," Cassie confirmed with a slight nod.

"That's the brief synopsis. Though it does get more complicated," she conceded. "I will break this down into phases to ease your understanding, and I'll review it at times to ensure you're following. If you aren't well rehearsed with the Bible, it's a lot to take in."

Maddie rustled, extending her neck forward like a giraffe as if this action would project her voice further into the front seat. The woman always ensured she was acknowledged.

"I've heard this all my life. As a kid, it seemed too heavy to comprehend. I do believe Jesus is the Messiah," she sighed. "But I suppose that while my parents forcing this idea down my throat daily instilled this belief in me, it almost turned me away."

Cassie turned toward Maddie, smiling empathetically.

"I understand, Maddie. I grew up in a small church, and I felt like, 'Why should I bother, when nobody can be perfect and sinless?'" Cassie related warmly.

"I think that our parents' generation was an era during which they saw the world changing, and they beat religion into their children out of fear. This turned many of their children away from God, and as they grew up, rebellion set in. For many, this followed them into adulthood."

"My upbringing was very protected," Cassie confided, now speaking to each of the girls.

"My grandmother wouldn't allow me to go to the mall until I was a senior in high school. I couldn't even listen to rock music in the '80s; I remember sneaking a radio onto the bus to listen to Duran Duran! I was just convinced I'd be sent to Hell for listening to worldly music!"

Maddie and Jules chuckled softly. Even Angie suppressed a small smile, Cassie noticed, as she glanced at her from the mirror.

"But the truth is, as I was growing up, I was just content with going to church on Sundays. I knew I didn't have the intimate, personal relationship with God that my grandmothers did. I just didn't know how or what this looked like. My church was too busy trying to scare the Hell out of us, literally," Cassie continued.

Angie piped up from the back, once again stunning the other three women.

"How could a God of grace, mercy and love allow such an outbreak of unbridled terror and bloodshed?" she inquired.

Cassie moved her mouth to speak, but Maddie responded first.

"God's very nature is to love. He shows grace and mercy, but He is a God of justice. Seeing the evil take place on this earth now, justice will be served. God wants no man to perish. Two particular verses about this spoke to me," Maddie began.

"In John 3:16, Jesus states, '*For God so loved the world that He gave His one and only Son, that whosoever believes in Him should not perish, but have eternal life.*'"

"But this is followed by John 3:36, '*He that believeth on the Son hath everlasting life: and he that believeth not the Son shall not see life; but the wrath of God abideth on him.*'"

Cassie beamed at Maddie, impressed with her friend's contribution to the discussion. The girls all knew that Maddie was familiar with the Gospel, but quoting scripture? That took everyone by surprise!

This is a person that openly wanted nothing to do with Christ.

"You're right," Cassie said, bobbing her head. "God is pure love, and because He loves us, He gave us a free will."

"Yes, it's instilled in me. I am just using my free will by living my will and wants, and I want to live my life without the intrusion of Jesus." Maddie concluded.

"There are so many other examples of people spared from the wrath of God. But the point is," Cassie elaborated, "God has given us warnings, signs, prophets and Gospel, and even with this, we have one final chance, after the rapture, to make it to Heaven. If you don't make it, you must be eager to go to Hell."

Maddie sunk back into her seat, occupied by deep thought. She exhaled a soft sigh.

"So, how do we read the Bible and comprehend it? It is brimming with old writings and difficult to understand," Jules asked, head cocking slightly to the right as she spoke. She was the picture of captivated.

"This can be tough at times," Cassie affirmed. "Just remember a couple of things. You can accept Christ, and the rapture can happen today, or perhaps you die tomorrow, and you are not responsible for learning the Bible."

"The thief beside Jesus on the cross simply said, 'Remember me,' and Jesus said, 'Today, you will be with me in paradise.' This said, I do urge you to dive in and start reading."

"The Bible is called the living Word because it can be tremendously powerful for you, the living. If you take advantage of it, it can speak to you and your situation. It comes alive in the sense that regardless of how many times you've read the same chapter, you can still hear something new. It's that amazing."

"There are deeper things. Let me explain," Cassie continued. "God put things we need to know in His Word. It's up to you to take the time to read it."

Let's go to the Word:

"Amos 3:7 states, '*Surely the Lord God will do nothing, but he revealeth his secret unto his servants the prophets.*' Proverbs 25:2 reads, '*It is the glory of God to conceal a thing: but the honor of kings is to search out a matter.*' Colossians 1:26 says, '*The mystery hidden for ages and generations but now revealed to his saints.*'"

"Once you know there is a treasure of knowledge and wisdom hidden for saints, it's up to us to find it," Cassie continued.

"In the New Testament, Jesus spoke to people in parables to make messages easy to understand, but He revealed the deeper things to His disciples."

No one knows the day or hour, but just as we anticipate the seasons, we will know the time frame of the coming of the Lord."

"As stated in Matthew 24:32-36, *'Now learn a parable of the fig tree; When his branch is yet tender, and putteth forth leaves, ye know that summer is nigh: So likewise ye, when ye shall see all these things, know that it is near, even at the doors. Verily I say unto you, This generation shall not pass, till all these things are fulfilled. Heaven and earth shall pass away, but my words shall not pass away. But of that day and hour knoweth no man, no, not the Angels of heaven, but my Father only.'"*

Cassie's eyes flickered over toward Jules.

"Granted, these are a lot of material and verses, but they will help you understand as we walk through all of this."

Twisting her body around, Cassie stared intently at Maddie and Angie.

"The attic at the gift shop," Cassie revealed. "I am making this a prayer room, and I want to stock it with all sorts of books. I will have books anyone can borrow, or even just take, if they see one that piques their interest."

Jules gaped. "Stop with the rabbit trails, you have me concerned. What will life be like if we are left behind?" she asked.

"That is a deep question and maybe time for some heavy notes," Cassey said. "Let's make a note for you to come back to this but I will include it in the study guide. We will call it, what to expect after people disappear.'"

"The study guide will be on the website to download for free. Oh, this reminds me of a poem I want to read to you!"

"Soon, very soon I'm coming for you,
It won't be long for I am pursuing you.
It won't be long that you have to wait
It's so close, you need to "save the date."
Refined in fire, my bride awaits
Glowing and adorned to take her place.
A persecuted church will be my mate,
To live in eternity in a righteous state.
Bid the earth goodbye, and look to the sky
This will be your last cry, and your very last night.

Are you looking for just one more sign?

It's beyond comprehension of your mortal mind!

I told you a mystery and I'll show you a light,

You know my voice, yet I'm out of sight.

The sound of a trumpet is your final sign

Don't end this day closed minded and blind."

CHAPTER 4

TRUMPETS AND THE LAST TRUMP

"I HEAR MURMURS ON every corner about the rapture," Jules started. "From social media, to videos and interviews; even people who aren't Christian predict something massive will occur soon!"

"But I worry," she fretted, small hands tightening around the steering wheel. "I know that we don't know when the rapture will begin, but could it be soon, with all of this going on? I've even heard whispers about dreams! One preacher is having dreams about a calendar."

Cassie nodded, empathizing with her friend's fear.

"I am not one to discern a dream," Cassie began. "Yet if it's the dream I think you are talking about, let's consider that the first part of his dream has already come true. But have you heard of the preacher's other dream?"

"It's in the middle of his sermon. Not many will listen to a two-hour sermon to hear a ten-minute dream," she remarked. "His dream declared that in September, people would be praying all month in great numbers, and toward the end of the month, the Heavens would open! He heard the Lord say three times, 'Come my bride.'"

"Then, he heard sounds as if thousands of shofars were blowing. Horn battle cries swirled in the air."

Maddie gasped, throwing her hand forward to grasp Cassie's shoulder.

"Wait, wait, we are near the middle of September now!" Maddie cried. "I'm familiar with these theories. I'm not saying that anything will happen, but let me explain why September could, one day soon, be rendered a significant month."

"Let's discuss these trumpets," she continued, releasing her deathly grip on Cassie's shoulder.

Cassie rolled her left shoulder a few times, wincing from her friend's physical display of enthusiasm.

"I know a bit about Jewish festivals. Tell the girls, and I will let you know if you are right," Maddie blurted out.

"'*Rosh Hashanah*' means 'the head of the year,' or the Jewish new year. In the Bible, this date is known as the Feast of Trumpets. The Feast of Trumpets, the Day of Atonement and the Feast of Tabernacles are three holy convocations, or 'festivals,' which the Lord commanded the Jewish people to observe," Cassie explained.

"Each date falls within the seventh month of the Jewish calendar, or *Tishrei*. The Feast of Trumpets begins the seventh month, as well as the Ten Days of Awe. These are ten days of repentance between the Feast of Trumpets and the Day of Atonement."

Cassie's blue eyes shone with mutual intensity.

"And that is why I am no longer looking for the signs of the times," she agreed. "I am not listening for the sound of the Trumpet!"

"What is a shofar?" Jules asked. "Is this the same as a trumpet in the Bible?"

"Yes, it's a style of trumpet. I have many notes in my book about this. I explain the Feast of Trumpets, the trumpets in Revelation 8 and 9 and the last trump in 1 Corinthians. It's a lot, and by this I mean, it's extremely dense information. It's not even something I'd like to get into right now," Cassie laughed.

"But I would love to share this information with you to read later, if you want to flip to the study guide. The 'last trump' could be at the Feast of Trumpets."

Maddie stirred again, popping her head between the driver and passenger seats.

"I've heard the terms 'mid-tribulation' and 'pre-tribulation.' When do you think this will happen?"

"Personally," Cassie responded, "I believe in pre-tribulation, and I hope I will provide enough information in my book to back up my reasoning. But it will take someone thoroughly reading the book and flipping through the study notes to follow. I'm praying that those who read my book will take the time to flip back and forth between story and study notes, to learn more about each topic."

"So this study guide is like Cliff Notes for the rapture?" Jules asked.

"In a sense!" Cassie chuckled. "The study guide consists of notes about many topics I thought would aid others. Whether readers need help understanding what is coming, or need help navigating through and getting saved after the rapture; people should not give up hope. My guide could help people decide what to do."

"Say the end of the world does come," Angie said, finally entertaining the concept. "How would someone know to find your book? How would one even know it contains vital instructions?"

Cassie smiled, enthused by the hardhearted Angie's newfound openness."Glad you asked!" Cassie encouraged. "Getting the book to as many people as possible would be wonderful, but distributing the message of what to do is my main goal. I want people to tell their family and friends, 'Do not take the mark or chip that will be required to buy or sell.'"

"Let's take you, Angie. You don't believe, but you have been educated about these matters enough growing up. If one day, you wake up and find legions missing around you, you may realize you were wrong. And hopefully, you will have my book, and you can then read it and share it with the people you know and encounter," Cassie wished.

"But, if you would acknowledge and accept Christ now, you would have fire insurance!" Maddie responded, with a grunt in her laugh.

"You can't exist in America, or even in most of the world, without learning of God and Jesus. In reality, you either haven't been exposed to enough truth to make a decision, or you have, and decided not to follow Jesus. Or, perhaps you did decide to accept Jesus," Cassie continued.

"The church body's mission is to steer the lost toward Jesus. But what happens when the rapture occurs, the church disappears and the lost are left alone? My heart longs for these people to come to Jesus. They are whom I write for."

"And I'm almost done writing. My study notes are complete, but my book itself is a work in progress. Here is a little bit about what we just discussed," Cassie said, flipping through her scribblings.

Let's go to the Word: Feast of Trumpets and the last trump in 1 Corinthians 15:52.

"A few verses form the basis of the dispute between when the rapture will take place. Will it be before the seven years, in the middle or near the end?"

"The verse 1 Corinthians 15:52 reads, '*In a moment, in the twinkling of an eye, at the last trump: for the trumpet shall sound, and the dead shall be raised incorruptible, and we shall be changed.*'"

Cassie paused, measuring her words.

"You see, at least two considerations are debated among scholars about when the last trump may take place. The 'mid-tribulation' idea would take place after the seven seals are opened and following the first six trumpets. I do not find this plausible," she emphasized.

Jules, looking quite puzzled, piped up.

"These terms are as foreign to me as an Indian speaking Mandarin in Australia!" she exclaimed.

Cassie chuckled.

"Yes," she agreed. "That's why I have so many notes in the study guide. And to speak a bit more Mandarin, the trumpet that is blown during the rapture could possibly happen at the beginning of the Feast of Trumpets."

"Interesting. Continue please," Jules encouraged, her interest peaked.

Cassie nodded, and began voicing a long winded and elaborate explanation.

"To understand if the 'last trump' at the Feast of Trumpets, go read the study guide online and the details of this festivals will be in #3,'" she concluded.

CHAPTER 5

THE SIGNS OF THE TIMES

CASSIE FELT INVIGORATED IN discussions about Jesus, and even more so when discussing Israel and how events were colluding. She continued speaking to the girls about Israel, pausing frequently to gauge their reactions.

Jerusalem was critical for the return of Christ. One of the main prophetic signs that civilization was nearing its end was the re-establishment of Israel, and Jerusalem returning to Jewish sovereignty.

"The Bible explicitly states that the Messiah is returning to Israel, and it's even more specific about the Mount of Olives. But certain events will take place first," she said.

"Israel's origins can be traced back to Abraham, the father of both Judaism, through his son Isaac, and Islam, through his son Ishmael. Abraham's descendents were enslaved by the Egyptians for hundreds of years before settling in Canaan, which is now approximately the region Israel."

Maddie eagerly jumped in.

"What is the saying about the 'signs of the times?'" she asked, eyeing Cassie.

"Good point," Cassie enthused. "Let me equate it to this. We have seasons of the year, and just like we don't know exactly when field flowers will be in full bloom, or when trees leaves will yellow and then brown, we know rough timeframes for these changes through observation."

"Similarly, the Bible contains many specific prophecies and signs. When these events take place, we know His return is close."

With a deep sigh, Cassie continued.

"The signs we're witnessing now, they seem so precise, and so close. We're looking at a tree with buds all over it, and we're compelled to think, 'they're nearly in full bloom. It's almost time for His return.'"

The girls all shifted upon hearing a faint murmur from Jules in the backseat.

"The comments all over social media and videos!" she quietly mused. "The chatter I've seen is because those who know, know what is going on."

Cassie privately smiled, noting Jules' growing interest in the conversation. If Jules understood more about Israel and its people, matters would grow clearer, she decided.

"Let me explain how Israel was rebirthed in a day, then you can visit the study guide for more details," Cassie started.

"The word 'Israel' comes from Abraham's grandson, Jacob, who was renamed Israel by God. The Jewish people have been in and out of bondage most of their existence. Other kingdoms have come and gone, and many other kingdoms have been determined to wipe Israel off the face of this earth, but no matter the circumstances, God prevails and the Jews come back strong. Finally, on May 14, 1948, David Ben Gurion declared the restoration of the Jewish State."

"Israel, in one day, came forth just as prophesied by Isaiah. Isaiah 66:8 reads, '*Who hath heard such a thing? Who hath seen such things? Shall the earth be made to bring forth in one day? or shall a nation be born at once? for as soon as Zion travailed, she brought forth her children.*' Just as it was prophesied, Israel was reborn in a day."

Let's go to the Word: Prophecy fulfilled that Jerusalem Restored into Jewish Hands

"The Lord declared in Luke 21:24, '*And they shall fall by the edge of the sword and shall be led away captive into all nations: and Jerusalem shall be trodden down by the Gentiles until the times of the Gentiles are fulfilled.*' In June of 1967, Israel miraculously defeated the superior Arab armies during the Six-Day War. The Jewish people took back the city of Jerusalem after almost 2,000 years, fulfilling this important prophecy."

"This is dense," Jules gaped. "These insights sound like a history lesson. Can you explain this in a manner that I can follow? What specifically can we expect after people disappear?"

Cassie nodded and reminded them, "You can review this in the 'study guide #2.'"

"I get on rabbit trails at times," Cassie acknowledged.

Maddie shook her head in rigorous disagreement.

"No!" the girl laughed. "You blaze your own maze in the forest and expect all the turtles, bears and porcupines to keep pace with you!"

"Understood. Back to the basics," Cassie shrugged. The woman continued with her story.

"After people disappear, events will occur which you have never experienced. All of life will be inverted overnight, and it will continue to change faster than you can keep up. The world will be chaotic, terrifying and almost unsurvivable."

"The economic implications of millions of people being raptured is hard to envision. Imagine those struggling now, during COVID. The government is paying out unemployment and stimulus checks, over forty-five million people have lost their jobs, and the unemployment rate has crept higher than the depression of the 1930s."

"If the U.S. banks and citizens have financial and foreclosure problems now, picture millions of American homeowners suddenly disappearing, never making another mortgage or rent payment again. What do you expect will happen when millions of business owners are suddenly unable to pay their bills? When their employees go checkless? When they can't continue providing essential goods and services?"

"Consider our federal government, which is already at the brink of bankruptcy. What will happen when millions of taxpayers are suddenly no longer paying taxes? What will happen to humanitarian relief groups and charitable organizations, which are primarily funded by Christian non-profits?"

"America houses a higher number of Christians than any other country, two hundred and thirty million. How could the U.S. possibly remain a global superpower, post-rapture? It's easy to predict how a single chip could be required to buy or sell, and how a one-world government and one-world religion will seize power."

"In the earth's downfall, one man will easily seize power: the Antichrist. He will rise, and most of the world will blindly or knowingly follow him as the world leader. Global despair will breed the perfect conditions for these events to conspire."

"And this was just a brief overcap," Cassie shuddered, cold suddenly.

"If you wish to dive deeper, I encourage you to. It's not a tough topic to comprehend, but it's more than we have time to discuss during this trip. I have notes on my computer, it discusses these brutal seven years, including a breakdown of the first three-and-a-half, and how they differ from the second three-and-a-half. It also elaborates on the wrath, the peace treaty, the Antichrist, the mark of the beast and more. Visit the study guide and go to #5.'"

CHAPTER 6

THE DRESS REHEARSAL

STEERING WITH HER LEFT hand, Jules suddenly reached over and grasped Cassie's arm with her right.

"This chip," she gasped. "Is this what they've been discussing on the news? The vaccination that could contain the chip? And how does this relate to the cashless society?"

Cassie shook her head slightly.

"It's behind the scenes. All of the details are being formed now, with their beginnings set in motion for when the time is right. I believe what we're witnessing now is a practice run," she explained.

"A dress rehearsal of sorts. Implement it now, in the test phases, and gauge how the public responds. Work out all of the kinks. Once the Antichrist orders remainers to take the chip, he will need everything working perfectly."

"I'll explain more of what will occur in a brief synopsis, and then tonight we can read my book notes on my computer for the finer and deeper details."

Jules nodded slowly, both hands secured on the steering wheel again.

"I'd like to hear about what happens after the rapture. Tell me more about what the world will look like after everyone is gone," Jules urged.

Cassie flipped through her notes, cleared her throat and started.

"I've told you girls a bit about this. As you know, a leader known as the 'Antichrist' will step up and command power. During this time, the planet will operate with a one-world government and a one-world monetary system," she said.

"Later, a one-world 'church' will form with the help of the 'False Prophet.' A peace treaty between Israel and her enemies will be signed, and the temple will be rebuilt. Yet this feigned 'peace' will only last three and a half years."

You can read more about this in Ezekiel 38 & 39 and in Daniel 9:26-27.

"There will be one hundred and forty-four thousand Jews, who God seals and protects to be witnesses," Cassie said, referencing Revelation chapter 7.

"These Jews will flee into the wilderness, most likely in Petra. Two witnesses will appear in Jerusalem and inform the Jews that Jesus is the Messiah they have been searching for. These two will serve as witnesses for three and a half years, at which point they will be killed."

"Revelation 11:3 speaks of these two witnesses," she continued, thumbing through her Bible.

"*And I will give my power unto my two witnesses, and they shall prophesy a thousand two hundred and threescore days, clothed in sackcloth.*"

"There will be a False Prophet who will denounce Christ. He will then deceive people into worshiping the Antichrist, and erect an image of him for people to worship. This is detailed in Revelation 13," Cassie explained, gesturing toward the book..

"These two will command all of the left behind to take the mark. Known as the 'mark of the beast,' the chip and the number 666, this mark will be required to buy or sell. The False Prophet, the Antichrist and their followers will attempt to kill all people who refuse the mark."

"And God, during this time, will pour out judgments which can be read throughout

Revelation. These consist of seals, trumpets, and bowls."

Cassie turned to meet Jules' gaze. Then, she craned her neck toward the backseat, making eye contact with Maddie, and then Angie, studying each lady carefully before continuing.

Sensing their stress, she explained the following horrendous prophecies to the girls delicately.

One-fourth of the world's population will die from war (Revelation 6:8). An earthquake will devastate the planet (Revelation 6:12-14). Something will fall from space and burn up a third of all the world's vegetation. A meteor will crash into the ocean and kill a third of the world's marine life. Another object from space will contaminate the water supply and poison millions (Revelation 8:7-11). Something will block out most of the sun and moonlight so that the days appear shorter (Revelation 8:12). Then, locust-like demons pour out of the earth and sting people like scorpions. The pain from their stings will last 5 months. Two hundred million riders on horse-like creatures will kill one-third of the people (Revelation 9:1-19).

"Three and a half years into the Tribulation, the two witnesses will be killed," Cassie continued.

"Their lifeless bodies will remain in the streets for three and a half days, and then they will come back to life (Revelation 11:7-12)."

"An asteroid will hit the earth and contaminate much of the water (Revelation 8). The earth will grow much hotter than normal, and earthquakes will be tremendous, destructive and unprecedented (Revelation 16)."

"A war called Armageddon will commence, and then Jesus will return with His church, setting His feet on the Mount of Olives (Revelation 19). Yet the Antichrist and his army will attempt to stop the return of Jesus."

"Revelation 19:19-20 reads, '*And I saw the beast, and the kings of the earth, and their armies, gathered together to make war against him that sat on the horse, and against his army. And the beast was taken, and with him the false prophet that wrought miracles before him, with which he deceived them that had received the mark of the beast, and them that worshiped his image. These both were cast alive into a lake of fire burning with brimstone.*'"

"Next will be a thousand-year reign and the judgment seat of Christ," Cassie articulated, emphasizing each syllable of these words.

Cassie's spiel was interrupted by a sharp inhale from a wide-mouthed Jules.

"Wait, pause! Hit the brakes and take a breath," Jules boggled. "This is so beyond detailed, and it sounds almost too strange to be true."

"I agree," Cassie sighed. "But believe it or not, this was a brief synopsis. The Bible describes these future comings in far more detail. One day, life will force people to read those scriptures like the daily news report, rather than as prophecy."

Jules nodded, her eyes still glazed over in confusion. "Could you explain that?" she asked.

"On it," Cassie agreed, opening her phone notes app to cite specific facts. Thus began her next explanation, during which she illustrated the following scene.

The books of the Old Testament are a blend of history and prophecy. Many of its books, when written, were prophecies to unfold, and since have come to pass. Now, they are history to us. John divided the book of Revelation into present, past and future when he wrote it on the isle of Patmos.

Emperor Domitian banished John to the Island of Patmos for preaching that Jesus had risen from the grave. They tried to kill John by boiling him in oil. That attempt failed, so the emperor sent John to the island. About 18 months later, Emperor Marcus Cocceius Nerva released John.

John died a short time later in AD 98, but while still on the island, God spoke to him and gave him visions. John needed to conceal the true meaning of these visions, so he recorded them in symbolism.

The contents of the book of Revelation will be uncovered when the time is right. Back then, the Romans may have read what John wrote and assumed he went mad. They may even have considered his contributions a fictional novel.

"Is that biblical?" Angie asked.

"Is it biblical that John went mad and wrote a novel?" Cassie laughed. "Of course not. I was explaining how severely the Romans misunderstood his writing. Yet if they had understood it, they most likely would have destroyed it."

Angie frowned in mild embarrassment, and collapsed back into her seat.

"Does this Revelation book include a timeline or an approximate date? When does the clock run out?" Jules asked eagerly. Her eyes bulged in excitement, as if a secret code were about to be revealed.

"Sorry Jules," Cassie shook her head. "Not even Jesus knows; only the Father in Heaven. We can rely on signs, and there is undoubtedly a heavenly clock. Add this to your list of extended studies when you have time."

"So, check out the study guide later on and read #5 if you want to know when the rapture will happen. Minus the exact date, of course!"

CHAPTER 7

I HAVE NEVER HEARD ALL OF THIS!

ANGIE AIRED HER THOUGHTS with a twinge of frustration, as if the discussion throughout the past few hours had been completely pointless.

"I am done!" Angie sighed haughtily. "No matter how many facts or scriptures you throw at me, I have made up my mind."

Cassie raised her eyebrows at this, her mind zoning in on her friend's use of the word "me." Angie felt personally attacked by this conversation, regardless of Cassie's intentions. And she felt this way despite having gone to church, read the Bible, and having parents who emphasized the importance of religion.

Maddie, acting as the mediator between them, quickly interjected, "Some of this rings a bell, but most of it is new. How come most churches don't talk about this?"

Cassie detected a note in Maddie's voice that revealed her softening heart. Maddie could become more willing to accept the Lord, Cassie thought. Her hopes, hard hit by Angie's defensiveness, again soared.

"Satan has a lot to do with this," Cassie said, selecting her words with care. She paused, cocking her head contemplatively, mentally preparing her next explanation. She would read an excerpt from her book, she decided.

Then, Cassie continued.

Throughout the ages, Satan's job has been to distract, lie, kill and destroy. He has hoodwinked many people. Despite there being a Christian church throughout the world and in each locality, his lies have consumed many confused souls. We're each responsible for deciding whether Jesus or Satan is the path to follow! Once you conclude the Bible is true, make a choice; to accept Jesus as the Messiah, or to keep embarking on the path toward Satan. Don't forget, if you don't choose Jesus, you are choosing Satan by default. Do not accept the mark, and fight for survival through the seven years, or die a martyr.

Jesus' disciples asked Him about the signs that would be precursors to His coming and the end of the age. Jesus' response is recorded in Matthew 24. There will be wars and rumors of wars. Kingdoms will rise against kingdoms; nations against nations. The Greek word for nations is ethnos, meaning ethnicity. Most of our wars today are racial wars. As I am writing this paper, I am in awe at the rate of the moral decline in our country. Christ foresaw that many will fall away from their faith, the love of many will grow cold and the world will have an increase in lawlessness. It's appalling to watch this unfold on the news today.

Following the rapture, or catching away, one of the first deception attempts will be from governments, trying to manipulate the public into believing that it didn't occur. They will describe the rapture as an "alien abduction," or some other peculiar rationale. They will do the Antichrist's bidding, as at that point, it won't be difficult for the Antichrist to gain followers. Those left behind already believed the Messiah wasn't real; it will be exponentially easier to deceive those remaining.

The initial hardship on earth will be a lack of food, violence, and brutality. These forces will be a battle to those left behind every day as they struggle just to survive. I personally anticipate power outages all over the world, and if that happens, you can't even imagine the chaos that will unfold. And soon after, money will be obsolete as they institute a one-world monetary system. You have been groomed to accept this for years! If you hope to survive, leave town and relocate to a remote area, preferably with a group of like-minded people. We are all a quest of Satan, and our world is falling to evil by the day. The devil is conscious of his fleeting time. He has long abandoned his ambition of overthrowing God. He tried that and failed repeatedly. His sole objective now is to drag as many souls toward the pits of Hell as he can.

Cassie continued, "Recognize that even Satan knows he has been defeated each time he has taken on God." She flipped forward in her Bible, her pointer finger sliding across the tops of the pages.

"As stated in I Peter 5:8, Satan continues to prowl about like a roaring lion. *'Be sober, be vigilant; because your adversary the devil, as a roaring lion, walketh about, seeking whom he may devour,'*" Cassie declared, her voice strong and full of conviction.

"He has given up the chase for victory. Satan's desire is to corrupt humanity as much as possible during his stint here, filling Hell with millions of souls. An eternity of agony awaits them, alongside him and his rebellious angels. He has read the Bible; he knows the end of the story."

Revelation 12:12 states *"Therefore rejoice, ye heavens, and ye that dwell in them. Woe to the inhabiters of the earth and the sea! for the devil is come down unto you, having great wrath, because he knoweth that he hath but a short time."*

If Satan knows the story's ending, then you should know it even better!

CHAPTER 8

WHAT IF I AM LEFT BEHIND?

ANGIE, WHO HAD BEEN intermittently listening to the conversation following her tangent, decided to play a card.

"So, if I am not a believer and I am willing to gamble, what do you mean by this 'martyr' thing? It appears to be a take-it-or-leave-it deal. If I am left behind, then everything you've said is correct. And I would be a fool to take the mark and go to Hell!" Angie scoffed.

"I mean, I am not sure I believe in Jesus, but I believe in Heaven and Hell! Tell me a little more about how I avoid 'going straight to Hell, not passing go and not collecting $200,'" she quipped, masking her anxious curiosity with a Monopoly analogy.

Cassie clutched the Bible on her lap, her other hand grasping her phone. She turned and handed the phone to Angie. "I assume you don't have a Bible app, correct?" she asked Angie. "Follow along with my phone as I show you these verses."

Maddie threw up her hand.

"This is getting too complicated!" she shrieked. "And look at poor Jules, she's been driving nonstop for hours. She should be a part of this. Let's take the next exit and grab some coffee. I'll drive, and Jules can use my phone for the Bible app."

"Your phone has a Bible app?" Cassie asked Maddie, smiling. "Does your phone have a Bible too, Jules?"

Maddie nodded fervently, and then moments later, professed, "Wait, no, I lied, but I can download it."

"I have a copy of the Bible at home. When it comes to this stuff, I'm not without hope, I just don't become overly invested in it. I attend church on both Christmas and Easter, as well as during funerals and weddings," she joked. "I even know about the 10 virgins!"

"What?" Jules asked. "Is this the parable in the Bible of the ten virgins who eagerly await the coming of the groom?"

"Are they all getting married on the same day?" Angie posed, interested.

"No, this story is about how some of us eagerly await Christ's return, while the rest remain unprepared. There are more details about this in my book, so maybe we can read it and discuss it later in the study guide #6: The parable of the 10 virgins: 10 virgins waiting for the bridegroom, 5 had their lamps full and entered, 5 were not prepared, and did not enter," Cassie responded.

The car whipped down an old country path parallel to the highway. Jules slowed to a snail's crawl, turning the car into the parking lot of a quaint country store called "Lucky's." Moments later, the girls shuffled out of the car and filed into the store.

A few minutes after, Cassie reclaimed the passenger seat, fastening her belt and peering around. All of us are in the car ready to go, we're just waiting on Maddie, she thought.

"Does Angie need to help Maddie with her bags? She will bring enough food to last us all weekend!" Cassie remarked aloud, eliciting a laugh from Angie.

Maddie then emerged, towing a mountain of concessions in her little arms. Upon a closer look, the woman was holding two cups, a bag of snacks and a few other items. She hopped into the driver's seat beside Cassie, stashing her drinks in the cupholders.

Jules snorted. "With you eating all of that, are we still stopping at the buffet in Fairfield? The town should be coming up soon," she wondered, now sitting in the back with Angie.

Maddie laughed at Jules' remark, adjusting the mirrors and slowly peeling the car away from the parking lot.

"Of course," Maddie cackled. "Just wanted a little something to nibble while I'm driving to pass the time." A little something? The girls all chuckled.

Cassie cleared her throat, ready to get the conversation started. "Take your phones, and go to page 847," she urged.

"What?" Angie asked, puzzled.

Cassie laughed and clarified that when they have time, they should go read the Book of Revelation, the last book in the Bible app, it will explain in several places what happens when you take the mark and what life will be like after the rapture.

"If you are left behind," Cassie reminded the girls, "Do not accept the chip; the mark of the beast. If you don't accept it, your road on earth won't be easy. You will have to go into hiding or become a martyr. Accept Jesus Christ as your Savior, and don't be afraid of being killed.

Taking the mark might ease your life for a few years but you will be trading a few years of convenience for an eternity of hell, literally."

"Provided I finish my book on schedule, you can read a full summary of the 7 years. Flip to the study guide #7," Cassie beckoned. "This section will provide a synopsis of the 7 years."

Cassie quickly explained the concept of a martyr, and Revelation's prophecy of a group of Jewish people who would be present as witnesses during the tribulation.

"Let's start at Revelation 6 verse 9, so scan to that. I've been asked, 'If I take the mark which is essential to my survival, can I still ask God for forgiveness?' This is an excellent inquiry, but no!" Cassie cried. "We accept Christ and put our trust in Him, believing that He is the Son of God. If you accept the chip, you are pledging the Antichrist as your Savior. You have sealed your fate forever with this deal. The Lamb will unleash His fury, and God will unleash His wrath."

Jules took a deep breath. "And I assume you are going to tell us all about the wrath of God and the Lamb?"

"Not entirely, but of course you will get a glimpse," Cassie agreed with a smile. "And if this piques your interest, you know to make a note to ask me for the details later on."

"It won't mean much to you now, but there are seven seals, seven trumpets, and seven bowls." In a confident voice, Cassie explained, "For those that don't believe there are consequences for taking the mark or don't believe Hell is a real place should read Revelation 14:9-11. '*And the third angel followed them, saying with a loud voice, If any man worship the beast and his image, and receive his mark in his forehead, or in his hand, The same shall drink of the wine of the wrath of God, which is poured out without mixture into the cup of his indignation; and he shall be tormented with fire and brimstone in the presence of the holy angels, and in the presence of the Lamb: And the smoke of their torment ascendeth up for ever and ever: and they have no rest day nor night, who worship the beast and his image, and whosoever receiveth the mark of his name.*'"

"The first bowl He pours out will be a terrible affliction of painful sores on their bodies," Cassie elaborated.

Jules glared. "I wonder if there will be more people accepting the chip than those declining it."

"I think many will take the mark," Cassie answered sadly. "It looks like we're being prepared for this as we speak; complacency training."

Cassie turned toward Angie, gently reminding her that if she accepted Christ as her Savior, the whole group could be raptured together.

"Maddie's got to do it first, but if she does, I will too," Angie smirked.

Cassie grinned inwardly.

"The interesting part is that there will be two people who never died; they were raptured up to Heaven in those days. There's no question that one will be Elijah, and some people think the other will be Enoch. Others believe Moses is the other, because God Himself buried him in death," she continued.

"That party believes God has kept his body safe to raise him during the tribulation as one of the two witnesses. Crucially, there was a meeting between Moses, Elijah and Jesus at the mount of transfiguration."

"What's your opinion, Cassie?" Maddie asked, turning toward her well-versed friend.

"I'm leaning toward Enoch and Elijah. The Scriptures clarify that all humans die once. The two witnesses will testify on earth and then will be put to death," she answered thoughtfully.

"Look! God allows His two witnesses to perish," Angie exclaimed, forever the contrarian.

"Good attempt, Angie," Cassie poked. "God will revive them after they have been lying in the streets for three and a half days. The people will rejoice when the two witnesses are killed, and they will share gifts to mark the occasion. But when God brings them back to life, He will take them up to Heaven in front of all. The Bible states that the whole world will observe this together. The technology necessary for that is now in place. All countries and religions."

Cassie continued, "Let's look at the Bible for further explanation, and also to review the marriage supper of the Lamb. And of course, you can read my study guide, #8 for martyrs, the 144,000, and 'great multitude.'"

CHAPTER 9

RAPTURE PARALLEL

JULES FELL SILENT FOR a moment, her eyes shining in solidifying realizations.

"So God is ensuring that all who wish to follow Him will have the chance to go to Heaven," she pondered. "Cassie, I understand that we don't know all right now, but do you have any concept of when the rapture will begin?"

Cassie jumped at this question, enthused to answer.

"Yes, He is, Jules!" she beamed. Her expression quickly morphed into stoicism. "And I do. I believe the rapture will happen at the beginning of the seven years."

Without missing a beat, Cassie expanded upon her answer. "And crucially, the rapture is not the same as the second coming. The second coming will occur at the end of the seven years.

The phrase 'second coming' is referenced over 1,800 times in the Bible. It is mentioned in twenty-three of the twenty-seven books within the New Testament, over 318 times, and Jesus Himself referred to His return twenty-one times."

"Did you count them?" Angie jabbed.

"No, I asked Google." Cassie sparred back.

"Angie, I think you need immediate proof of what I'm asserting. Just for your sake, and yours alone, I am going to leave important verses in my book for you to read along the way. Others can read these, or skip them altogether and follow along with the storyline of the book. I will dedicate the entire purpose of 'Let's go to the Word' to you, Angie!" Cassie declared, her gaze boring holes into Angie.

She was fed up with the woman playing adversary to her every word, and frustrated! Cassie swarmed in frustration, but her resolve to get through to her friend was unwavering. She silently prayed for additional patience, and to find the words to touch Angie's heart.

Jules, on the other hand, remained visibly intrigued.

"Will people just disappear without a trace, or could somebody actually see them soaring away into the sky?" she asked.

"No," Cassie responded. "It will happen in the 'blink of an eye,' as stated in the Bible. Have you seen movies or read books where clothes and jewelry are scattered on the floor, almost as if they were discarded in a hurry?"

"I still find this hard to believe!" Jules puffed, her eyes wide set in surprise. "I've known people who have said they are saved and are headed to Heaven, but it remains a struggle for me to comprehend the notion of a rapture."

Cassie pointed out that although the Bible did not contain many accounts of people being raptured, there are still a few examples.

Angie exhaled from the backseat, offering tangible proof she was listening after all.

"I'd heard of folks being raptured in the Bible, though I had never taken it seriously," she softly admitted.

Cassie pointed out that Enoch, Elijah and Jesus had all been raptured.

"I've said more about this in 'the study guide online #20,' the Old Testament parallel of the rapture. Enoch, Elijah and Moses. Maybe read more about it in the study guide online."

"Oh, before I continue, I want to share this poem," Cassie voiced.

"Longing for the day I'm able to see,
My savior standing in front of me.
I will bow before him on bended knees
So, I make my choice to serve and believe.
Down here we live a fast-paced life
We make excuses for sin and not living right.
It's easy to live out of mind, out of sight
But what if this was your last night!
Would you leave in peace or with a fight?
What angel will come and take you away!
When you stand before God, will you leave or stay?
When he opens the book of life, what will he say,
Will your name be missing as he turns you away
Or will this be the beginning of your eternal days
Well done my good and faithful servant
This can't be bought and you cannot earn it.

It's easy to say a prayer and speak in faith

How will you respond when death is in your face;

Will you stand with authority or tremble and cave?

You accept by faith what was given by Christ

He made the choice and paid the price.

Will you live in peace, or struggle in strife?

You have the free will to accept eternal life

What would you choose, if this was your last night?"

CHAPTER 10

BACKSLIDDEN, LOST OR RIGHTEOUS?

MADDIE THEN SPOKE, HER voice inflections spiking with anxiety. She admitted intense nervousness, as she had refused to accept Jesus as an adult, festering childlike bitterness toward her parents.

"I felt so much anger toward them that I completely shut out their teachings. Will I be able to experience the grace of God if I accept Christ now?" Maddie fretted, an iron grip clasping the steering wheel.

"And Angie!" she cried, eyes flicking toward the mirror. She glimpsed Angie's crossed arms in the backseat. "Could she really just change her mind, now, after never believing before? Would that be enough to absolve her of all the wrong she's done over the years?"

Angie's breath caught in her throat. Was her future already sealed?

"Seriously?" Cassie cooed, reaching to gently pat Maddie's shoulder. "Do you believe that the God who sacrificed His Son for you will abandon you after all the effort He put into bringing you into His presence? Do you really think that you're damned just because you took longer to arrive? The one thing about God is that His love for us is limitless; this concept is beyond any human understanding."

"He reminds us that when we repent, and accept His Son Jesus Christ, He will forgive our sins and renew our spirits."

Cassie then cracked a joke, her dry sense of humor on full display. She explained that though they were not the worst of the worst, all are sinners.

"But if you turn around and accept the Lord, you could be rapture ready for tomorrow, and you will have a one-way ticket to Heaven," she emphasized.

Maddie mulled over this for a few moments. What could be the fate of someone who accepted Christ as a child, but then led a life of debauchery?

Then, speaking up, Maddie confessed, "I don't think I ever self decidedly accepted Christ, growing up in church. I honestly just went for the punch and cookies, and to play while my parents were in the adult sermons."

"Are you wondering if every individual who has proclaimed Jesus as their Lord and Savior will be taken to Heaven in the rapture?" Cassie intuited.

Then, Cassie drew in a deep breath.

"Would you believe me if I told you this is a hard one? I am not sure I can answer it," she answered genuinely. "I can provide you with an array of scriptures that explain why only the righteous will go, and then I can give you verses that speak of grace and the forgiveness we receive. I can't judge the sincerity of another person's heart."

"If you sincerely accept Christ as the Son of God and entrust Him with your life, then you are saved. When in doubt, let's go to the Bible," Cassie said, relieved to reference the book.

"Christians tend to disagree on this subject, but most opt to remain silent to avoid offending one another. Will only those who live according to the word of the Lord ascend in the rapture, or do those who were saved but still succumbed to the passions of the world go as well? Here is a great verse that stimulates thought. It's one of the many parables to explore."

"Matthew 24:40-42 reads '*Then shall two be in the field; the one shall be taken, and the other left. Two women shall be grinding at the mill; the one shall be taken, and the other left. Watch therefore: for ye know not what hour your Lord doth come.*'"

With a twinge of sadness, Cassie acknowledged that even though she didn't know all the answers, one thing was certain.

"As you reflect on your life, ask yourself; am I living for God or am I living for the world?" She posed this question solemnly, her blue eyes locked on the road ahead.

"The world is growing more immoral, and we are being taught to overlook wrongdoing, and swallow the bad as acceptable and reject the right as wrong. Our attitudes and perspectives are being manipulated. They say that if you put a frog in a pot of warm water and gradually increase the heat, the frog won't notice the change. The pitiful frog will gradually acclimate to the water until it eventually dies."

Maddie exhaled and then spoke in earnest, "I would rather live for God and be judged by the world, than live in the world and be judged by God."

"Good point," Jules agreed.

Grasping her Bible, Cassie then stated, "As we get closer to the end, these seven deadly sins will become increasingly visible."

Revelation 9:20-21 proclaims, *"And the rest of the men which were not killed by these plagues yet repented not of the works of their hands, that they should not worship devils, and idols of gold, and silver, and brass, and stone, and of wood: which neither can see, nor hear, nor walk: Neither repented they of their murders, nor their sorceries, nor their fornication, nor of their thefts."*

Maddie responded with firm conviction, her voice resolute as she declared her goodness. "I am a vastly more moral person than most people today."

Cassie smiled at that.

"Instead of providing my opinion, I give you the Bible. Then, you can figure out what works for you," she suggested to her beloved friend.

Let's go to the Word:

Matthew 7:21, *"Not every one that saith unto me, Lord, Lord, shall enter into the kingdom of heaven; but he that doeth the will of my Father which is in heaven."*

Ephesians 5:27 *"That he might present it to himself a glorious church, not having spot, or wrinkle, or any such thing; but that it should be holy and without blemish."*

CHAPTER 11

LUNCH BREAK!

"I COULD EAT ANYTHING right now," Jules whined, grasping her stomach. As if upon command, it growled.

"For the Word," Cassie breathed quietly.

"What do you mean?" Jules asked, lifting her brows.

Maddie turned the wheel, pulling into a gravel parking lot just off the freeway. Cassie, in her own world, illustrated the feeling of being "starved" for knowledge of Jesus, who is also called the Word.

Halting her ramblings, Cassie looked out the window and noticed the outside world. The suburban was parked outside a big, proud buffet hall.

"Who has been here before? This is the best buffet on this side of Texas! The food is simply divine," she grinned excitedly.

"That's what I've heard, but I've never been here before!" Jules chirped, peeking her head up front. "Let's scarf down some food and make haste to Dallas so we can check in. I'm craving a swim tonight to loosen up my tight muscles after hours in the car."

"Hey Angie, I'm gonna be at the bar lifting weights, you in?" Cassie asked, searching to ease the tension with her friend.

"We're not getting into any arguments about politics or religion, are we?" Angie posed, kicking at the rocks under her boots rather awkwardly.

"Deal!" Cassie agreed. The women met eyes and laughed, clearing the air.

Maddie hopped out of the car, turning to face the girls as she locked up. "Don't forget your masks, let's not give anyone the wrong impression!"

The girls fought through legs long limp from their journey, stumbling clumsily through the door of the countryside restaurant. Then, the smell of home cooked southern cuisine wafted into their noses. The air was rich and decadent.

Cassie scanned the room, noting the tables were still spaced at fifty percent capacity. The plates, on the other hand, were piled high.

The buffet was otherworldly. Widemouthed dishes nested warm, crispy and moist foods with mouth watering aromas. Everything was cooked or baked or browned to perfection. Small town, hidden gem dining surrounded the women; these delicacies must have been cooked by every grandmother in town!

The four girls filled up their drink cups, placed them at an empty table near a window, and rushed over to grab their food. Cassie mouthed a silent prayer to God; she couldn't believe the buffet line was still open, given the strict protocols businesses were following!

One by one, the women walked along one side of the aisle while waitresses served from the other side, their faces elongated by plastic shields that were longer than usual. The COVID restrictions are ever-changing, Cassie thought to herself.

The women had to remain masked until they took their seats.

From the front of the entree line, Cassie glanced over and spotted Angie's tall stature. The woman was at the dessert bar before she got in line!

"What are you doing?" Cassie asked, a hint of surprise edging her voice.

"As you kindly reminded us, we don't live forever!" Angie poked. She gazed at her food lovingly. "I'm not taking any chances, so I'm having dessert first. Check out these homemade chocolate and coconut pies."

"Are you eating both of those?" Jules laughed. "I'm taking a slice off the meringue, so it's just one piece of pie. I'll go back for the blackberry cobbler with ice-cream for dessert."

The girls headed over toward their table, carefully towing small mountains of food. Moments later, Jules cleared her throat between bites and asked, "So, what is the game plan for when we get to market?"

Cassie released a loud, hearty laugh. The other girls glanced at each other, their faces filled with confusion.

"What is so funny?" Jules asked.

"That's Cassie," Maddie offered, recalling the abrupt chimes of her friend's giggles every time she thought of something funny. "Cassie gets overcome by laughter from her inner thoughts. Soon, she will be laughing too hard to tell you the story she is amused by!"

"Well, before that happens, let's have it. What on earth is so funny?" Angie asked, leaning forward, her face in her hands and her elbows planted on the table.

"Have I told any of you about having 'the talk' with my son?" Cassie asked, forcing her humor filled voice to relevel. Her three friends shook their heads minutely.

"We went on a trip and stayed at our timeshare around a year ago. I was hanging out at the restaurant while my husband and son were swimming. Well, my son strolls in, and I don't recall how, but we got to discussing the end times. Noah knows God and knows about the rapture."

"I looked at him and said, 'Noah, you and I have never discussed what happens after the rapture. I think it's time; I ought to explain the consequences for those who stay on earth and are not spared by the rapture.'"

"And at his young eleven years of age, I could see the most precious, inquisitive look on his face. We talked for around an hour, and I gave him as much information as I thought he could comprehend."

"The following morning, I rose early and began working on my laptop while sipping coffee. After a few minutes, Noah showed up. I asked him why he was awake so early."

"He told me he was giving thought to what we had discussed the previous night, and he wanted to know if there was anything else I needed to explain. This puzzled me. I recall wondering if I'd scared him a bit, or if he was really just that invested in the details of the end days!"

"So to clarify, I asked him, 'Do you mean about end times? I think that is about it.' Then, he looks up at me with the most serious little stare, and he asks, 'So, was this the talk?'" Cassie let out a giggle, and her friends immediately joined in with amusement.

"I laughed so hard!" Cassie continued, once she managed to control her laughter. "My son, without a doubt, believed that we'd just had the long-awaited 'talk' that every parent needs to have with their kids."

"Too cute," Maddie murmured, a smile spreading across her face. "I can visualize his face, trying to mask his relief that he had avoided the notorious 'talk,' only to discover that it was just postponed!"

The girls all broke into laughter again.

"Okay, let's talk about the Dallas trip," Cassie said, reeling them back in. She recalled the original purpose of their trip: they were heading to Dallas Market to pick out gifts for their store.

Jules was the first to speak. "I think we should be conservative with our purchases! We don't know how this year's economy will go," she advised. "We can always place orders to be shipped later in the year and restock as needed."

The other three agreed with this precautious strategy, and for several minutes, they continued chatting about their favorite brands and entertaining what might be trendy this year. They made their list and checked it twice, so to speak.

Cassie, a meticulous planner by nature, smiled inwardly at their unified game plan. One must have a tactful approach to get the most out of shopping at the Dallas market, she thought.

The women quickly finished up lunch and stood up, grabbed their purse and the check. They were eager to complete the final hours of the drive to Dallas.

Jules and Angie beelined toward the restroom while Maddie and Cassie lingered around their table, waiting for their to-go ice teas.

To Cassie's surprise, Maddie faced her and said, "Hey, I have a question for you about the 'salvation' thing. What if I am feeling, you know, like…"

The woman suddenly fell quiet, noticing Angie approaching behind Cassie.

"Nevermind, I'll ask you about this later. We have plenty of time on the trip to talk," she finished quickly, just as Angie drew near.

"Hey, Cassie, don't you and I need to go pick out bags for the store?" Maddie asked, louder now.

Cassie coughed, concealing a small chuckle at her friend's terrible attempt at inconspicuousness. She could have just come forth and asked her question, Cassie thought to herself. Before she could play along, Maddie turned toward Angie, yelling, "Shotgun!"

Angie playfully scurried past them, shouting behind her shoulder, "Not if I get there first!" Then, she raced toward the car, unaware that she had no competition.

Maddie giggled, facing Cassie again. "I knew that would get her away for a moment. I have to say, Cassie, I tuned you out during the first part of the conversation. But honestly, I know where your heart is. I want some notes to review what I shut out. Would you print some pages for me, one day, while we're at the hotel?"

"I'd love to review them while we're here. Maybe during my 'me time' while I'm taking a bath."

"Absolutely!" Cassie flashed a radiating smile. "I will print my 'study guide in depth, #5,' which is a synopsis of the seven years. And I will print something I know you've heard before, but I guarantee never you've never seen it as a line-item, easy to read list. It's in the 'study guide, #9' explanation of the seals, trumpets and vials or bowls that will be poured out during the tribulation."

Maddie and Cassie exchanged nods, and then bolted to the restroom for one last trip before leaving.

"Hey Cassie," Maddie started, drying off her hands. "Won't the Antichrist have a sidekick called the 'False Prophet?'"

"Yes, he will," Cassie nodded. "The False Prophet will be a religious leader who will denounce Christ. Revelation 13:12-15 states that the False Prophet will have the same power as the Antichrist, and he too will perform miracles, convince people the Antichrist is the Messiah, and worship of the Antichrist in the temple."

As the two rushed back to the car, Cassie noticed Jules and Angie sitting on a nearby bench. The four exchanged excited smiles, as Cassie motioned they would be there in a moment.

"Who are these two witnesses?" Maddie asked, now unbothered by Angie's proximity. "I have heard of two or three different men who will come back. Are you familiar with this?"

"Yes," Cassie smirked, "This must have been one of those early car conversations you tuned out. I will print this as well. Keep in mind this is still in rough draft form. But I actually have a section in my study guide I am calling 'Who are the two witnesses, #10.'"

Maddie continued the conversation seamlessly, without missing a beat. "I have a vague memory of hearing about four horses, but I can't place their importance," she probed.

"This is all listed in chapter six of the Book of Revelation," Cassie responded, fastening her seatbelt just as the wheels started turning. "Do you want a quick rundown of the four horses?"

"I wouldn't mind hearing this," Jules readily agreed.

Cassie dug through the bag at her feet and plopped her Bible in its rightful place: down onto her lap. "The seals are part of the wrath that will be poured out during the seven year tribulation," she began.

"There are different levels of wrath in the book of Revelation. First will be the seals, then trumpets and then the bowls or vials. But there are also the thunders, which are not described. God told John to seal this up and not write about it," Cassie revealed ominously.

In the backseat, Maddie's eyes widened.

"Chapter six of the book of Revelation details the seven seals. The opening two verses depict the first seal, the 'white horse' and the coming of the Antichrist to conquer. He will wear a crown and promise lies of peace; this will be a deception to bring war against the saints."

"The second seal will bring forth the 'red horse,' and with it war will soon come, according to verses three and four. The third seal, explained in verses five and six, speaks of a 'black horse' that will bring famine to the entire planet. Once the war and mass destruction have ended, the survivors will be forced to struggle to survive with very little food."

Cassie breathed a sigh as she continued. "The fourth seal, verses seven and eight, describe the 'pale horse,' bringing death to a fourth of the planet. The fifth seal, verses nine and eleven; martyred believers will call for justice. They will be in Heaven, under the throne, and given white robes with a single command, 'rest.'"

"The sixth seal, verses twelve through seventeen. The sun will turn black, the moon red. Mountains and islands will vanish and there will be great quakes."

"And the seventh seal, Chapter 8:1, foresees silence filling Heaven for a brief time before this last seal brings about the 'trumpet judgments,' followed by the bowls or vials," Cassie exhaled.

"Well, I feel like we dove weeks into a Bible study within a few hours! This is something I beckon people to study, especially those who may be left behind in the rapture. Lost souls will especially need to hear about the judgements, so they can view. 'Study this in depth, #11' for the judgements; the 'great white throne' and 'eternity.'"

CHAPTER 12

THE ANTICHRIST AND THE WRATH

JULES NODDED ARDENTLY. "*I* am following all of this now. It's helpful that you have reviewed it a couple of times. The repetition helps me understand. It seems the Antichrist is the main player in the end. Can you expand a bit more about him? Why is he the one in power? Do we know who he is right now?"

"Nope," Cassie responded. "We know he has to be living right now, but we don't know who he is. In Revelation 13:2, Satan bestows his power upon the Antichrist. This is deeper than making him powerful; it's giving the man his own supernatural power."

"The Antichrist is also referred to as the 'man of sin,' 'the son of perdition' and 'the beast.' He will rise after the rapture takes place, and he will be brilliant; a great political man with unprecedented charisma. While the world is in chaos, he will promise false hope. He will both claim to and succeed in bringing economic stability to the world's monetary system, and he will bring world peace, while masking a true intent and deceiving many."

"The Antichrist will control the world's economy," Cassie proclaimed, thumbing through her Bible. "He will '*force all people, great and small, rich and poor, free and slave, to receive a mark on their right hands or their foreheads, so that they could not buy or sell unless they had the mark, which is the name of the beast or the number of its name,*' (Rev 13:16-17)."

"Satan endows him with his power. He gives to him his throne. And he also gives to him great authority. He will convince the Jewish and Arab nations to sign a peace treaty that will bring the rebuilding of the third temple," Cassie declared, waving her arms to paint points the way a conductor might.

"His accomplishments will be so spectacular that many will believe he is the actual Messiah. He will claim to be God, and many will worship him."

Let's go to the Word, Revelation 13:13; He Will Display Miraculous Power, as it is stated: he will *perform great signs, even causing fire to come down from heaven to the earth in full view of the people.*

Jules lifted her brows. "How will the Antichrist get Satan's power and authority?"

Angie murmured in agreement. "Is this the same as selling your soul to the devil?" she asked.

"Times a thousand!" Cassie roared, enthused to elaborate to open ears. After a moment of thought, Cassie realized how much time her explanation would take.

"Tonight, at dinner, I will fetch my notes and we can discuss this," she decided. "I put this in my study notes."

"Let's go study this in depth, #12." The Wrath. And, "Let's go study this in depth, #13." How did Satan get the power to give to the Antichrist?

With an elongated sigh, Jules said, "I wonder if the man knows he will be the one right now."

"I am not sure about that," Cassie pondered. "I haven't read anything that leads me to believe the Antichrist knows he is about to step into power. It's only around the middle of the tribulation that Satan will give him the full extent of his power."

Cassie continued, "The Book of Revelation, from Revelation 6:1 through 19:21, provides specific details for what will happen during the tribulation. Chapters six through eleven give details of the first half, or the first three and a half years, and chapters thirteen through nineteen cover the second three and a half years. The seven year tribulation will begin with the breaking of the seals, but you can research this later on."

"It's in the 'study guide online, #14, the Seals being opened.'"

The extent of these details dumbfounded Jules. She realized she would need to study this material in depth.

"I'm noticing I need to get up to speed," she gasped. "I will begin carving out time to read the Bible when I get back home. So, I suppose I'll just open up page one and start reading?"

Cassie's lips curved into a smile as she responded, "I would start in the New Testament."

"In the beginning, God created the Heavens and the earth," is the opening statement of the Old Testament. Then covers the creation of Adam and Eve and other significant events that span 4,000 years.

Malachi's prophecy, the last word from God to Israel, brings the Old Testament to a close and ushers in a period of four hundred years of divine silence.

In the New Testament, they document the life of Christ from his birth to his crucifixion and resurrection.

The birth of the church can be traced back to Acts. As you read, you'll discover how the disciples risked everything to share the message of Jesus Christ with others. The last book of the Bible, Revelation, was written by John, who was exiled to the island of Patmos by Emperor Domitian, expecting he would die there. The last surviving member of the original 12 disciples was John.

"And the book?" Jules asked, "How did they retrieve it?"

Cassie continued, saying, "They actually released John from prison, and I think he completed it around 99 A.D."

"John's estimated death date is around 100 A.D., which would be in the first century. Historical accounts suggest he passed away because of old age in Ephesus, a city in Asia Minor," she elaborated.

"So," Jules tried again, "Where should I start in reading the Bible?"

Cassie smiled. "I, personally, would want to know more about the man who gave his life for me. Matthew, Mark, Luke and John are the gospels. They all tell the story of the life of Jesus, some with some different details."

Cassie's face lit up as she continued, "The Bible is our blueprint for life; it's a source of hope and a direct connection to God. When you read it, you can feel the Holy Spirit in your heart, providing guidance on how to live a moral life, to forgive, to have faith and to be accountable."

As she spoke, Cassie's face displayed great contentment. "I could go on and on, but the Bible is the sustenance of life, like the food we eat, the air we breathe, and the water we drink. I can't explain it, but I hunger for the Word of God just as extremely as I hunger for food."

Jules fell silent. Minutes passed, and the smooth, barely audible sounds of Angie's earbuds were all that could be heard.

Then, Jules finally asked, "Is this what you meant when you said that Jesus is a part of your daily life?"

Cassie faced the woman. "How would it feel if your children or husband did not communicate with you daily? If they were not enthusiastic about having a relationship with you? I know we can't see God, but we can sense Him through the Holy Spirit. He's our comforter," she voiced.

It seemed as if Cassie's words touched a personal spot for Jules, and she was curious as she asked, "How do you spend time with Him?"

"In prayer," Cassie answered.

"God has given us free will; He is not forcing us to choose Him. His hands created us, so it's no wonder He desires us to choose Him. Believing that Jesus is the Messiah will breed inside us a passion to learn more about Him, and that will grow into a powerful love."

Then, Cassie's eyes narrowed, and she shrugged her shoulders, saying, "Choosing to not accept Christ is choosing Satan by default."

"I have wondered how many tears God has shed as His children have passed away, rejecting His love. How much hurt will He suffer as He watches during the seven year tribulation, while the people He created deny Him and praise Satan and the Antichrist instead?"

Jules shook her head dejectedly and whispered, "That is sad."

Then, the two spotted the girls' hotel alongside the road. Jules blinked and began pulling the steering wheel toward the right, exiting gracefully.

"I have another question. Actually, I have many more questions, but let's discuss this later," she said.

The two women in the back giggled with excitement.

"Are we almost there? Are we there yet?" Maddie and Angie chattered consecutively, as they always did after any long drive.

It was almost happy hour for Maddie and Angie, and the women were all checked into the hotel in two adjoining rooms.

Cassie and Jules made their way to the pool, the sound of their flip flops smacking against their feet, while Maddie and Angie beelined toward the bar for happy hour.

Angie leaned in toward her closest friend of the bunch, her voice low, and asked Maddie, "What do you think about all of this?"

"Honestly, I do believe everything she said. I've spent a lifetime so upset with my parents that it's caused me to doubt God's goodness." Maddie spoke with an air of dismissiveness, as if she somehow still rejected God with the same disregard she had for her parents.

"Angie, what questions linger in your mind? What is it that has caused you to doubt?" she probed.

"I was raised with the same beliefs as my parents, so when things went wrong, I directed my anger at God," Angie scoffed bitterly.

Maddie raised her glass, chuckling. "Cheers to living our life without parental or spiritual authority!" Angie tapped her glass on Maddie's with a loud "clunk."

"Amen to that, sister," she hooted. Already having had a bit too much to drink, the two girls crossed the line with the religion talk.

Between gasps, Maddie continued, "And I don't need Cassie shoving religion down my throat like my parents did." Angie laughed, uttering again, "Amen, sister."

Angie tapped Maddie's glass once more. Then, she paused, shaking her head.

"I take that back, I disagree with you there," Angie admitted. "Cassie has pressured neither you nor me. She was just there to answer questions. Other than being annoyingly adamant about her beliefs, she hasn't actually pushed us."

"Sure, but she adamantly prays for us," Maddie retorted. "Anyway, another bottle? Red or white to finish the night?"

Across the hotel, Cassie was relaxing, lounging by the pool with her eyes gently closed. She abruptly opened them, feeling a splash of cool water hit her feet.

"Hey, one more question: what began the idea of your book?" Jules shouted, playfully pushing water toward Cassie. Cassie inhaled deeply, rubbed her tired eyes, and smiled down at Jules.

"It's a book for you," Cassie grinned, her blue eyes twinkling with joy.

Jules chuckled, recognizing the humor in Cassie's teasing words.

"I wrote this for you, Maddie, Angie, my family, and for everyone who will take the time to read it. While people are aware of Jesus and the rapture, few are equipped to handle the aftermath of being left behind," she began.

"I ask people all the time if they know how to advise their family and friends on survival and redemption if they were to be left behind. Not many have been able to provide the right answer. The only answer is to never accept the mark, the chip, or whatever else they choose to call it; the mark of the beast, which will be mandated to purchase and sell items. With no guidance, those left behind will struggle to understand they can still have a chance to make it to heaven."

Jules vacantly stared at Cassie. Her eyes were set in an empty, dissociated gaze, her mind whirring away, but not really grounded in the moment. With a slow, deliberate nod of her head, Jules finally responded, "Okay."

Then, she spun around and swam off.

Moments later, Cassie heard Jules walking by. Jules was wrapped in a towel, her sandals planted back on her feet. She inquired of Cassie if they should go to the room, as it was late.

"Sure," Cassie agreed. "Seven a.m. will arrive quickly, and we have an extended day ahead of us."

The next morning, Jules woke to the boisterous blaring of the hotel alarm. She turned and sat up suddenly, noticing Cassie was gone. A chill ran down her spine, and she frantically wondered, "Is this it? Have I been left behind?"

Jules cleared her head, laughing at herself. "I'm worrying too much; she's probably downstairs, having her morning coffee and checking emails." She picked up her phone to send her friend a quick text, just to ease her worries.

Jules anxiously peered down at her phone, her heart still racing, as she texted Cassie. "Have you already had breakfast?" Seconds later, Cassie responded, "Nope, just having coffee and waiting for you guys."

Jules giggled to herself. "I am taking all of this way too seriously!" she mused as she grabbed her clothes and headed toward the shower. A bit later, Jules checked her reflection in the mirror and headed downstairs, wondering how late the other girls stayed up.

She dialed Maddie with no answer. She tried Angie, who responded immediately. Angie answered the phone with a quick "hello." Maddie could hear the woman fiddling with her phone from the other end; she was playing a phone game undoubtedly.

"How much longer until you come down for breakfast?" Jules asked.

"I need forty-five minutes or so. Maddie just now hopped in the shower, so I'll tell her to put a rush on it," Angie responded. She ended the call.

Jules headed downstairs on her own and stumbled upon Cassie, who was rapidly typing.

"Morning. What are you working on?" Jules inquired.

"Top of the morning to you," Cassie sang. "With my book finished, I've been pondering whether I should be explicit in writing out each Bible verse, or just leaving a few for readers to reference. If I were left behind, I would want this book to provide all of the answers."

"Yet if I read it beforehand, that could be too much to take in," Cassie debated with herself.

Jules peered over Cassie's shoulder, peering at the dimly lit computer screen. "What's the next part? It says 'overcomer,' what is that?"

"There are many verses where we overcome the wrath of God; 'to those that have an ear, let them hear,'" Cassie quoted. "And I'm glad I have your ear," she joked dryly.

Jules studied Cassie, her own face expressionless. "That's sort of why I arrived a bit earlier than you expected. Can we talk?"

"Of course," Cassie nodded.

Jules inhaled slowly. "This morning, when I woke up and my alarm went off, you were not in the other bed. And for a moment," she breathed jaggedly.

"For a moment, I was scared. I was lying in bed, and I felt like I was talking to God. I mean, I heard nothing back, but I spoke to Him."

Cassie cocked one brow. "So, you were praying?" she asked.

Cassie's stomach had butterflies, hoping that Jules was going to ask what she had been anticipating.

"I don't know if I did it right, or if I said the right words. But I want to know Jesus like you know Him," Jules professed, her mouth set in a small smile, her eyes wet.

Cassie's eyes began to brim with her own tears. "You want to accept Jesus into your life?" she asked slowly, locking gazes with her friend.

Jules nodded, minutely yet confidently. "Yes, yes I do. This is truly what I want. I may not know much. I mean, I know I can't educate others on 'end times,' after that trip yesterday," she said, laughing.

"But I know I want a relationship with Him."

Jules and Cassie prayed together. Then, Cassie walked her through the sinner's prayer.

Cassie taught Jules how to ask for forgiveness and allow Jesus to take control by becoming the

Lord of her life. Jules closed her eyes in earnest and prayed with all her might. In her heart, she fully believed that Jesus was the Son of God. He was born of the virgin Mary, crucified, raised on the third day and seated at the right hand of the Father.

Jules held her head low the entire time, tears streaming out of her closed eyes. Her heart and soul felt full for the first time in her life.

Then, the two were quiet. The silence was profound.

Cassie finally opened her mouth to speak.

"Are you going to share the news with the other girls?" Cassie asked.

"Yes, but I'd rather let them know tonight, if that's alright," Jules decided. "I want to take some time for myself and for Jesus today. I want to enjoy my peace, before I tell them, because after I do, I'll have to face Angie's wrath."

With a throaty laugh, Cassie agreed.

"Yes, you'll be spared from the wrath of God in the tribulation, but we'll both have to deal with the wrath of those two," Cassie joked back, noticing Angie and Maddie walking towards them.

Cassie said, "I will print some notes on wrath for the girls to read later. Angie wants you to believe she is not listening, but she is. I think these three topics would be a good read for them in my study guide."

"Let's go study this in depth, #15." To those that have an ear, let them hear.

"Let's go study this in depth, #16." Eternal rewards for the overcomers.

"Let's go study this in depth #17." Seven church warnings in Revelation chapters 2-3.

CHAPTER 13

NOT YOUR AVERAGE DAY

THE FIRST DAY OF the market had arrived. Cassie craned her neck around like an owl, searching for Maddie and Angie, who were about thirty-five minutes late for breakfast. She spotted the two girls scrambling into the restaurant.

"Maddie made us late," Angie blurted.

They scarfed down breakfast and beelined outside just as the shuttle pulled up. Maddie turned to her friends, inquiring if they had their rolling bags.

Angie nodded rapidly. "Yep, I have it. Let's just go!" she exclaimed.

"On the road again, I can't wait to get on the road again," Angie sang as the girls jumped on the shuttle bus and headed a few blocks away, toward the market.

Maddie rolled her eyes and chuckled, "Angie, if you don't stop singing, we won't make it to market; we'll just end up on tour!"

"I need to call and check in at home," Cassie said. "The reception is not that pristine at the market, and I just wanted to say hi to my little guy and my husband."

"What about Kate?" Jules asked.

"Oh, we spoke earlier this morning. I sent her a list of things to work on while I am on the trip, and we text constantly," Cassie responded.

To this, Angie smiled. "Cassie, it is so cool that you get to work with your daughter," she said softly. "I want to call and check on my family too, and let them know that I'll touch base this evening when we get back to the hotel."

The women each turned to their phones and spent a few moments chatting with their loved ones.

Maddie's conversation was quick and short.

"How is your husband?" Cassie asked her. Maddie snorted, replying quickly, "He's doing great. He's eating, drinking and being merry, and occasionally yelling at the TV during the football game!"

Per usual, Angie was the first to jump out of her seat, her excitement bubbling like a kid in a candy store. After disembarking from the shuttle, the four stepped into a large revolving door and pulled on their masks. Then, they marched toward the check-in counter to collect their badges and catalogs.

Following their well-coordinated plan, they each conquered a specific region of the market, purchasing the items they anticipated would become hits. In addition, they gathered catalogs for future purchases. Each girl made a list of stores to return to and snapped photos of potential ideas to discuss on day two.

When she parted from the registration desk, Cassie shouted, pointing across the market's horizon, "You know I am headed to my favorite area." Speeding up her walk, she declared, "I will cover the gourmet food areas and Christmas gifts."

If Cassie had her way, the store would pervade with notes of pine and gingerbread yearlong. Her friends joked that she celebrated Jesus' birthday all year long; she agreed that the peace and joy it brought her was undeniable.

In the final quarter of each year, Cassie dedicated most of her time to events for her full-time business. Thanksgiving weekend marked the end of her work year, and she felt immense relief. December was her month of rest and relaxation.

Cassie would say, "I need a month-long vacation to recoup from the events." A full month of no emails or phone calls. Just being at home, where she could experience the warmth of a cozy fire and the comfort of a hot mug of cocoa.

"It's my time to decorate my home, watch Hallmark Christmas movies and bake cookies," she'd coo. Her eyes turned starry with the excitement of filling her home with cheerful music, scents of freshly baked cookies and twinkling decorations.

Each winter, Cassie was finally able to take a break from the hustle and bustle of everyday life. Spending sacred quality time with her family during the holidays was what made it complete.

The girls had a wonderful time shopping. The hours flew by, and before they knew it, it was late afternoon, when they'd scuttle to meet for lunch and share their findings. Some days, at noon sharp, they would munch on an array of foods, exchange stories and compare discoveries. On other days, they kept walking, placing orders and pocketing catalogs until they'd finally decided upon enough orders for Four Southern Chicks to thrive throughout fall, Christmastime and spring.

Paddy's was the restaurant of the market, the warm aroma of savory dishes filling its air. The walls were scrumptiously lined with a potato bar, pasta bar, salad bar, homemade pizzas and Italian food. Each girl stacked her plate high, checked out at the register and sat down with the others.

Angie said, "Okay, let's hear the list. Cassie, what goodies did you stumble upon?"

At this, Cassie's face lit up with a grin. She pulled out her phone, thumbs twiddling across her screen as she scrolled through the pictures. "I couldn't resist buying these little guys, my fall and Christmas gnomes. Look at how cute they are," she sighed, her voice colored with delight.

"I know I went a little overboard with snow globes, but I just couldn't resist. The ones shaped like old console TVs are nostalgic. Remember those bread bowl candles we were searching for? Well, I found them, and I also stumbled upon these adorable burlap shopping bags!" Cassie rejoiced. Her enthusiasm was an art of persuasion, and everyone hopped on board for the next item.

"Let's discuss the paper gift bags," Maddie contributed. "I was thinking we could opt for the small ones as gift bags and offer the large ones for free with a hundred-dollar purchase. Though the bag costs only ten dollars, plus shipping, I'm confident that women will spend more than that just to get the bag for free. Despite the ten percent loss, our average sale will rise significantly, making it a worthwhile trade-off."

Then, Cassie changed pace, her tone clear and sweet. "Can we bless our food before eating?" She bowed her head in prayer. Around then, with her eyes closed, Maddie heard a pause in the prayer.

She waited for a second; perhaps Cassie was mentally preparing a long prayer of thanks for their trip, their food and their business.

Several long moments passed. Nothing. Maddie slowly opened one eye, and then immediately opened the other. Jules and Cassie were missing.

A minute ago, Cassie had begun murmuring her prayers. In the next, she and Jules vanished. Bodiless clothing draped floors and tables across the restaurant. Silence devoured the building; Maddie could hear the erratic pace of her terrified heartbeat.

Then, the building erupted in feral screams. Anguished sobs surrounded the girls, only two now. Others fossilized in confusion and fear.

She turned toward Angie, her own heartbeat now pounding in her ears. Maddie knew what had just happened. In that single moment, she experienced every physical and emotional sensation one could experience.

Then, she gasped as if a lightning bolt hit her chest. She could only utter a single sound,

"Angie." After that one word left her mouth, she was speechless. She began hyperventilating. Oxygen kept escaping her. She frantically scanned the room and was met with mirroring images of other people, frantic.

People kept screeching, faces red and twisted in sheer terror. Others paled, vacantly looking around; lost geese in a hailstorm.

Angie's voice welled in panic as she repeated, "No, no, no!" Maddie's cries filled the room, her hollow sobs echoing off the walls.

The girls met eyes, the sorrow behind each pair unmistakable. They had been left behind.

Maddie sighed shakily. Her voice came out as a whisper compared to the loud roars of the oblivious crowd. Angie's voice was soft as well as she asked, "Do we tell them, and will they believe us?"

"We both had doubts about it," Maddie trembled. "No, I believed, but I just couldn't accept it."

The restaurant fell into chaos. Wide-eyed remainers struggled to understand what happened. Others knew. One lady cried a guttural scream, "My girls, they're gone!" She fell to her knees.

The room, once bright and pleasant, was suffocating. The air dripped in sorrow as remainers grieved the vacant seats.

Maddie snatched both their purses up quickly, ripping through them to pinpoint their phones. Angie gestured to the backpack, rolling cart and clothes. "Leave them here and let's go!"

Before leaving, Angie faltered, lingering by the clothes. She leaned down, flipping through them. "Here they are, their wedding rings," she breathed, quickly tucking them in her back pocket. She gripped Cassie's cross necklace and hurried after Maddie. Angie grabbed Maddie's arm and said, "I grabbed this jewelry because it has sentimental value."

This meant something when nothing felt valuable anymore. Following Angie and Maddie, the restaurant emptied out as people entered the massive Dallas Market atrium. Carts and clothes scattered every corner. Cell phones sounded all over the floors, left to ring unanswered. But what struck the two girls the most painfully was the sight of empty strollers.

People waited in line to leave. The shuttle buses were in formation in front of the building, and people boarded the buses, but some were driverless. A sign hung from the breezeway, displaying different bus routes to varying parking garages or hotels. Angie grabbed Maddie's shoulder, pointing toward their shuttle's windshield.

"No driver," Angie remarked. "We can walk. Let's just get back to our hotel, grab our stuff and get out of here as fast as possible."

As the parking lot erupted into total anarchy, the girls bolted toward their hotel two blocks away.

A few minutes later, they stood at the window of their eighth-floor room. They gazed down below, overcome by a silent awe. The freeway and feeder roads they'd just driven across were now wilderness. Some cars were wrecked, others abandoned. Glass and metal shavings decorated the pavement.

The girls began moving. Maddie entered Cassie's room through the connecting room.

Angie shouted, "We don't have time to pack it all. Just grab the basics and let's get going!"

Maddie called back, "I'm just grabbing Cassie's laptop and her Bible; we're going to need them!" Angie looked puzzled for a second before then her face fixed in clarity. She responded, "Good idea. I have the keys and phone chargers."

The girls didn't spare the time to collect their clothes or suitcases. Checking out of the hotel was pointless at this stage. The business credit card was on file, and a monetary issue was the least of their concerns.

"How will we make it home with all these wrecks?" Maddie posed, her voice wavering. Angie, anxious and uncertain, suggested, "We can get to Dallas' edge and then take the back roads."

"If the back roads are blocked, I'll go through the grass and ditches if I have to," she planned. Angie glanced at her phone to assess if a Google route was an option.

Neither girl had not called home; their surging adrenaline had suppressed such thoughts. As they rushed toward the car, they both desperately dialed their husband. Angie's husband, Alex, answered on the first ring. Alex asked her why she hadn't responded to his dozens of calls, which were sent straight to voicemail.

"We've been rushing to leave Dallas," Angie explained as the girls tumbled into the suburban. "My phone has been on, but it hasn't even rung!"

Angie's voice broke as she assured her husband they were already on their way home. Weary, she tried three times to reassure Alex, "I know what has happened, and I will fill you in when I get home." Yet nothing she could say would ease the terror in her husband's voice.

Maddie felt her throat close up when she dialed her husband's number and was met with the absent sound of ringing. She tried to call again while she sped across the road. This time, the only noise was the robotic greeting of his voicemail.

Maddie fumbled through her bag for Cassie's phone. The bright light of the screen illuminated her face, revealing many missed phone calls. She noticed none of the calls were from Cassie's husband, daughter or son. This gutted Maddie for reasons she didn't understand.

A few minutes later, Cassie's phone rang again, and Maddie could feel the vibration in her palm. A contact name appeared, "John/shows." Maddie was very familiar with this friend.

"Cassie, is that you?" the voice shouted into the phone.

"No, Cassie is gone. It's Maddie."

The other line fell silent for a moment, and then John asked, his voice heavy, "Has it happened? I knew. I knew that if I couldn't reach Cassie, the things she had been telling me had become reality. Is this what she's been trying to tell us?"

Maddie's small voice again trembled, tears gushing down her cheeks. "I'm afraid it is, but we have some good news. Cassie didn't leave us ill prepared." She told John she'd get back to him, and right before hanging up, she yelled, "Keep me posted, John."

"Don't hang up just yet, please," John pleaded, determined to keep Maddie on the line. "I have no idea what to do or where to go."

"Due to the accidents, the trip back from Dallas will probably take seven hours. Do you know Cassie's residence?" Maddie inquired.

John responded slowly, "I know where she lived." Upon the last word, his voice fell deep; desolate.

Maddie sighed in agreement. "Let's meet there tonight, at midnight. Just a warning, there might already be other people at her house."

"How do you know they will come to her house?" Angie probed.

"The solutions to the puzzle are in her book," Maddie elucidated to both Angie and John. "She claimed that God was the one who had given her the inspiration for the book. If her family or friends were to be left behind when the rapture occurred, she left them with clear instructions on where to find a poem. She claimed it held instructions for this day."

"Simple," Maddie mused ironically. "Nothing Cassie did was simple, but she mentioned this could be her life's work."

Angie snapped her head back. She recalled a poem with instructions for this day, mounted in Cassie's entryway. Very few people were aware of that. Cassie's remaining family and friends were bound to show up to her house in pursuit of that paper.

Hours later, on their way back to Houston, the girls passed through Navasota. It was there that Maddie offered to drop Angie off at her house, because she needed to stop at home first.

Angie again dialed her husband, Alex. After several rings, he answered in a panic. "I have been calling and calling!" he fretted. "Are you still okay?"

"I am okay. Listen. I don't have time to talk. We are almost home. But listen closely," Angie instructed. "My phone is almost dead, and I need to charge it. I need you to go to Cassie's house and into the backyard workshop. You'll find a spare key hanging from a large thermometer on the wall. The key opens the front gate, but not the back door. Then, go to the front and enter through the gate. When you walk in the front door, you will see a small frame with a poem, just to the right of where she hangs her keys. Grab it and keep it hidden until I arrive."

"A poem?" Alex asked, bewildered. "I need to secure a poem?"

"I am having trouble hearing you. Reception is spotty," Angie said.

"She knew this day was coming?" Alex asked.

Angie, still trying to hold a broken conversation on a dying phone, responded, "Yes, millions knew this was coming. People like us called them 'crazy fanatics' and 'Jesus freaks.' We wanted all Christians to be banished from the earth. Well, we got our wish. But Cassie believed in the rapture's coming enough that she left us instructions."

"And she didn't think to warn us?" Alex asked bitterly. He was angry and hurt; none of this made sense.

"I told you, I will explain it all when we get there. Cassie told us she was even working on a book, and I have it. We grabbed her computer from the hotel before leaving. I love you. I will be home soon," Maddie promised. "But I need to go. My phone is going dead, and I want to charge it while I still can."

They drove south on 45 toward a small town, plotting to take back roads to get home. The usual one-hour drive from Dallas to Corsicana took three hours. The journey from Dallas to Houston should take three-and-a-half hours with no stops, yet the traffic jams would make this trip run close to seven hours.

Angie nervously tapped across her social media pages while Maddie drove, dread heavy in her chest, as she anticipated what her friends might be posting. Time seemed to stand still since the rapture had taken place, though it had only been a few hours ago.

The clock struck five o'clock, and the girls' hearts sank. Would they ever make it home? On social media, the reports of airplane crashes seemed to stand out amidst the countless car crashes.

People were already breaking into the stores, shattering glass and grabbing whatever they could find. Thieves freely roamed the streets, openly claiming jewelry, cell phones, purses and wallets that were lying around, their owners raptured.

Angie abruptly broke her silence. "Look, Mary posted that all banks are closed! They have already deactivated ATMs to prevent a run on cash!"

"Another friend posted a photo of the grocery store, with police cars parked along the front. They are open, but only allowing a few people in at once to prevent any potential looting. Hundreds of people are gathered in a line," she continued, her anxiety budding. "*The Post* noted that people are so angry, they are breaking into physical violence!"

Angie was rampantly scrolling through webpages and alerts when an unusual noise interrupted her. Was this an emergency alert?

One after the other, all four phones began blaring. But the message contained more than just words; it contained something else entirely.

This message contained an eerie voicemail icon, blinking, beckoning her to tap on it and listen.

The text on the message read, "This is the emergency broadcast system. This is not a test; I repeat, this is not a test." Then, a second message materialized. "Press one to access voice messages."

Angie activated the voicemail.

"This is your regional representative. It is universally known that we have experienced a terrible event which has impacted our country and the entire world," a computerized, female voice began.

"People everywhere have disappeared with no explanation. Our investigation has begun, and officials worldwide agree, with absolute certainty, that aliens have abducted our missing population. We have taken the necessary precautions to prepare for the days ahead, and we will continue to update you through this same channel. Every time, you will be required to affirm that you have heard the message. This will ensure we are communicating properly with everyone remaining."

"After hearing this voicemail, please input your full name, address and phone number in the 'response' bar. By confirming that you have received this message, we can keep an accurate toll of those who are unaccounted for, and of those who are still here."

"We will swiftly post the names of the missing on our website. There, you can search for your loved ones. We understand the importance of locating loved ones or confirming their absence. You may search for updates on our website at WHOknewit.org."

The voicemail ended as abruptly as it began. Angie stared at Maddie, her face torn in hesitation. "What do you think? Should I submit my information?" she asked, uncertain.

Maddie quickly agreed. She explained that she wanted to make sure people knew she was still alive, in case they were looking, and suggested they should check the list for their own loved ones.

Angie typed in her own information and then took Maddie's phone to do the same. Yet Maddie's phone blocked her from inputting a response until she had listened to the voicemail.

Maddie responded with a curious, "That's interesting." She then dismissed her suspicions, gesturing for Angie to press play on the voicemail and fill out a response. Over the next few minutes, Jules' and Cassie's phones beeped continuously with incoming messages. To maximize battery life and avoid the incessant beeping, Angie shut those phones off.

She tucked them away in the console. But after five minutes, the two phones came alive with the same sound. Angie lifted one phone, and the notification that appeared read, "Attention was required."

"Okay," Angie wordlessly agreed. She sounded the message, and following its conclusion, she wrote "RAPTURED" in big, bold letters next to Cassie's name. She hit send.

Almost instantaneously, the phone sounded. "Ding," it screeched. Angie's response was invalid.

"Try again," Maddie suggested. "This time, plug in 'disappeared.'" Ding! Invalid response.

"Alright, one more time," Angie sighed. She typed out "unknown" and hit send.

That response didn't do the trick. The phone, seemingly alive and watching, then instructed Angie to just record her own address. She input her address in the field, and ding! Her response had been recorded.

Angie glanced over at Maddie. "They will record Cassie and Jules as officially missing."

Maddie exhaled. "Aside from that... we haven't even talked about the obvious. We have been left behind!"

Angie gasped, their dire reality striking her tenfold. "This all feels like a bad dream. But it's okay," she soothed herself. "We are going to wake up tomorrow, get dressed and go to the market for a second day."

Maddie leaned across the middle console and smacked Angie in the back of the head. "You need to wake up!" she cried.

She glanced at Jules' phone, which was squealing demandingly. She eyed the alerts of sixteen new messages and twenty-three missed phone calls. "Maddie, did you notice how the messages didn't show until we ran the updates?"

Angie nodded and took the phone from Maddie. Hesitantly, she typed in Rick's number, Jules' husband. The line began ringing. After a moment, she heard the voice of a frightened man.

"Jules, where are you?" Rick asked.

"Jules... is gone," Angie responded slowly. Before she could finish explaining, he interrupted in a panic.

"The kids have vanished into thin air! And I got this message saying millions were abducted. What is going on?" Rick shrieked.

"I wish I could explain it all," Angie empathized, her voice a mere whisper. "But I can tell you that Jules and Cassie are safe. They were not abducted. They were raptured."

Rick scoffed, his volume hiking. "She didn't believe all that stuff."

"Apparently, Cassie reached her. Cassie and Jules shared a room on our trip. Cassie was writing this book about God and the rapture, and they spent hours talking about the intricacies of this book. At some point, Jules must have accepted Christ," she responded.

"You mean to say that Jules went from not believing in a God to believing in Jesus, within twenty-four hours? And that was enough to ensure her entrance to Heaven?" Rick posed, his voice dripping with defensive sarcasm.

Angie inhaled deeply, calming her vexed nerves. Striving not to snap at Rick, she retorted, "Well, it was that or aliens!"

Calmer now, she continued, "Cassie has been working on us for years. We are meeting at her house tonight at midnight. Do you know where she lives?"

"No," Rick replied. "Send me the address by text message."

Angie's hands moved swiftly as she tried to make the most of the fading phone signal. She sent the text, and Rick one last phrase from Angie before the phone call went quiet. "Get to the poem. It will clear up any confusion."

"What is she talking about?" Rick thought.

In the car, Angie leaned her head against the passenger window. "I can't bring myself to speak to anyone else. My mind is foggy," she said softly, closing her eyes. "It feels like days have passed since we left Dallas. Since all of... this... happened." The woman fell silent, trying to make sense of it all.

Maddie glanced over at Angie. She looked so small; so exhausted. This resonated with Maddie heavily. "Why don't you just open her computer, glance over a few pages and see if anything stands out?" she suggested.

Angie nodded, sitting back upright in her seat. She opened the computer, where the book was immediately visible on the screen, as if Cassie herself was whispering, "Welcome."

The font became more pronounced as Angie navigated the document, pausing at Cassie's recent revisions in the "Books in Heaven" section.

"What's the section called?" Maddie asked impatiently.

"Seriously, I am looking, and you demand quick answers!" Angie barked. "She was writing about the books in Heaven, and as expected, our names are not explicitly on here. She suggested we should all just keep watch, pray and look for His return. Practice a life of righteousness."

Angie exhaled, her voice level. "I remember her saying that if we were to be left behind, it wouldn't be too late to make things right."

Maddie, too, remembered this. "She said she would save us a seat at dinner," she chuckled tearfully.

Angie smiled, her own eyes brimming with tears. "'The Marriage Supper,' as she called it."

Maddie gave Angie's hand a reassuring squeeze. "We will be fine. We know not to take the mark, and now we will finally accept Christ. We are going to make it to that dinner, or at least in time for dessert."

Angie squeezed Maddie's hand in return, cleared her throat and began reading aloud.

"Let's go to the Word: Books in Heaven."

"Different books in heaven are important to have your name written in. It's discussed in the Old and New Testaments. In Daniel 7:10, it reads, 'A fiery stream issued and came forth from before him: thousand thousands ministered unto him, and ten thousand times ten thousand stood before him: the judgment was set, and the books were opened.' The book of life is mentioned in Revelation 13:8. 'And all that dwell upon the

earth shall worship him, whose names are not written in the book of life of the Lamb slain from the foundation of the world.' Just as your name is written in the book of life and you go to heaven, if it's not written in it, then you go to hell. *Revelation 20:15 explains, 'And whosoever was not found written in the book of life was cast into the lake of fire.'"*

"Let's review the books mentioned in the Bible."

"Let's go study this in depth: #18 Books in Heaven."

"Cassie noted, here, that this was one of her personal favorite sections!" Angie interjected.

"Let's go study this in depth in the study guide from the website, #19: Watch and Pray!"

"Well, Maddie," Angie began, "It's quite clear our names were not written in the Book of Life, and we have not been watching and praying. But didn't Cassie tell us that we have another chance to make it to Heaven, now that we've missed the rapture?"

"Yes," Maddie agreed. "I remember much of this information from my upbringing, so I anticipate a bit of what is coming. But I am so glad that we have her computer. I bet we will find more when we get to her house."

"So, we have a chance?" Angie asked again. A drop of hope began welling up in her chest.

"We do, but it's going to be hard. We must stay together, pull our resources together and work together. Read some more; we still have a couple of hours to drive," Maddie urged.

Angie nodded. "The next thing she wrote was something about 'as it was in the day of Noah.'"

"Oh, yes!" Maddie exclaimed. "That is how our world has felt lately."

"I will read you this brief section. But you know all the in-depth studies she talked about putting at the end of the book. We have a lot to study," Angie mused. She bowed her head toward the laptop and began reading.

"Let's go to the word: As it was in the day of Noah."

"'But as the days of Noah were, so also will the coming of the Son of Man be.' Matthew 24:37."

"This warning from Christ should serve as a sober reminder to our generation of the evil and rebellion we experience today as compared to Noah's day. Hebrews 11 is the Faith Chapter, and Noah is noted for his courage and trust in God, even when he couldn't make sense of what was to come. Read Hebrews 11:7. He completed the ark and entered with his family and the animals, the door closing behind them."

"Noah stands as a symbol of hope and salvation. Noah and his family stepped through the door to be preserved from the flood, and we need to enter through a door of salvation to be redeemed. *John 10:9 states, 'I am the door. If anyone enters by Me, he will be saved and will go in and out and find pasture.'* It feels *like our society is changing every day. Genesis 6:5: 'Then the Lord saw that the wickedness of man was great in the earth and that every intent of the thoughts of his heart was only evil continually.'* But the Lord still waits. *2 Peter 3:9 states, 'The Lord is not slack concerning his promise, as some men count slackness, but is longsuffering to usward, not willing that any should perish, but that all should come to repentance.'"*

"Study guide information for later: the #20 Old Testament picture of the rapture. Enoch, Elijah, and Moses, as well as other Old Testament saints, were delivered from the wrath."

CHAPTER 14

HOLY SPIRIT, PRESENT OR NOT?

ANGIE FOLDED THE LAPTOP so that it was slightly ajar and gazed out the window. She released an elongated, sad sigh.

"I'm still processing this all. I'm trying to wrap my head around how God found a way for His people to be rescued, and we simply went on without Him," Angie admitted. She felt suffocated by the tremendous weight of shame.

Maddie grew somber. "I am the more guilty one; but you know what? I know God still loves us so much," she mused.

Angie's brow furrowed in confusion. She inquired, "How could you be so sure?"

"He created us, and even though we don't always make the right decisions, He still loves us," Maddie explained.

Angie opened the laptop fully, and after a moment of scrolling, she extended her index finger toward a section about the prodigal son.

"I think that is us," Angie contemplated. She began reading the notes aloud, experiencing the reality of the story coming to life. "The following section appears to delve into the mystery of the Holy Spirit, and whether He will be present after the rapture, Cassie believed He will be."

Maddie's voice brimmed with concern as she exclaimed, "Oh, I hope so; we need Him!"

"Cassie left a short verse and then detailed notes for us to examine. Some believe that the Holy Spirit will remain on earth during the tribulation, while others think He will leave," Angie explained. She began reading once more.

"This belief is based on 2 Thessalonians 2:7. *'For the mystery of lawlessness is already at work. Only he who now restrains it will do so until he is out of the way.'*"

"It's explained in the study guide, #21. Will the Holy Spirit leave the earth at the Rapture?"

"You can also study this in depth: #22 Prophecy of Joel and the Pouring Out of the Holy Spirit."

Maddie interrupted Angie. "The Grand Parkway exit is in sight; we just need to keep up this pace, and we'll be at Cassie's house in twenty minutes or less," she said.

"I see. Are we leaving our cars at our homes, or taking them with us tonight?" Angie asked.

"Let's not linger; let's go straight to her house and get someone to take us. We'll get them tonight, in case something happens," Maddie decided. "I will ring to check if Alex and Rick have gotten to the house with no problems."

Maddie inhaled deeply and dialed her husband's number one more time. Mark's phone didn't even ring; it went directly to voicemail. Her fingers trembled as she hit "end call."

"What is your gut feeling about Mark?" Angie asked cautiously.

"My intuition tells me he will be alone in the house, typing on the computer and watching the game, with a glass of wine nearby. One glass leads to the next, and then the whole bottle; sometimes even two. And then, he'll be too tipsy to type, so he'll start singing karaoke instead," Maddie joked emptily. As she spoke, she privately prayed for his well-being.

"Mark could have easily dozed off while watching baseball in his man cave," she continued to rationalize. "During the week, he works so hard that he tries to make up for his preferred pleasantries in the early hours of Saturdays. Yet by midday, he has the same schedule."

Maddie's heart ached to believe that he was asleep. But truthfully, she was torn, equally hoping he was in Heaven.

Angie saw through Maddie's humor. She tried to console her friend, telling her that soon, they would be back home, and that she and Alex would go with her to check on Mark.

Angie picked up her phone and remarked, "Speaking of, I need to call Alex, since we are almost at Cassie's house." She scrolled through her messages, searching for her husband's contact photo.

"Angie, do you understand that we still have a chance?" Alex asked over the phone. "Despite our mistakes, God is still with us."

"Yes!" Angie agreed, her anticipation building as her house moved into line of sight. "Tell me, who have you talked to? Who is in the house? Who is not there? We have so much to catch up on, and I can't wait to see you and fill you in. We are making a beeline for the house, and on my way to check on Mark, I have to pick up my car."

"One question at a time, Angie," Alex calmed his wife. "Slow down; your adrenaline is racing."

"We passed the house, but there is no place to park," Angie fretted. She motioned for Maddie to drive ahead and park beside a neighbor's house. "There are no lights on, so it's probably safe to assume nobody's home."

"Henry is walking out to meet you," Alex told Angie.

"Henry, of all people, is still here?" Angie gaped. Maddie's jaw dropped.

"Hold on," Maddie interrupted, "How on earth did he miss the rapture?"

Henry approached the car just as the girls were getting out. He thrust his arms out, engulfing Maddie in a giant bear hug. "Are you ladies talking about me?" he asked.

"Yes, I want to know how you are still here!" Maddie interrogated him. Angie nodded her head in agreement, equally perplexed.

Henry breathed an embarrassed sigh. "Well, the secular world has gotten the best of me. Girls and drugs were too tempting to ignore. I wrongly assumed that I had an endless amount of time to live my life. I told myself, 'Enjoy the world and just ask for forgiveness when the time comes!' Clearly, I was wrong," Henry inhaled unevenly.

"I made a reckless decision. I waited too long, playing a deadly game of Russian roulette with my own life." He hung his head in shame.

These words struck Maddie as familiar, like something the old Henry would say; not the new one. Maddie pulled her friend's nephew into her side, tugging on him with her arm around his neck.

"No need to worry; we're all in this together," she pacified him.

Henry's solemn face suddenly broke into a grin. Proud, he declared that he had taken over Cassie's bedroom and made it his own. Pre-rapture, he had lived in a cramped apartment with two roommates. Now, he was too afraid to return.

Angie, who had her eyes trained on Henry, felt a force crash into her. Her husband had sprinted toward her, grabbing Angie and holding on for dear life.

"I didn't want to tell you on the phone," Alex gasped, "But your parents are gone, as are your sister and our three boys!"

Angie smiled, visibly relieved that they wouldn't endure the coming years. "I figured as much; I kept looking at my phone, hoping for a text from one of them, but nothing. I am not saying I am glad you were left behind, but I am glad you are here."

"Let's get inside!" Alex urged the group. "We have quite a few things to do tonight."

The four walked up the driveway, and Alex pointed to Cassie's cars. "These are up for grabs," he remarked. "My cousin's friend, John, is here, and he claimed this one," Alex gestured. "I have my sights set on the suburban."

"Why do the boys need a car?" Maddie wondered.

Henry quickly explained that John's car had been making strange noises for a while, and just as the rapture occurred, he was involved in a collision at a red light. Henry's own car, he described, was completely crunched in a pile-up on the freeway. He'd left it there and began a three-hour trek to his family's home.

Then, Jules' husband, Rick, emerged from around the corner and approached the party. His expression was contorted in a devastating mix of mourning, fear and relief.

Now unified, their faces all turned toward each other. They traded heavy and pained expressions.

Tears welled up in all pairs of eyes, and the group locked in a train-embrace, arms all wrapped around each other. They held each other tightly. It felt like a funeral of sorts, yet more extreme, because the living felt they were dying inside.

And then, all at once, the atmosphere shifted. The air grew lighter. Together, they felt hope.

Rick interrupted the moment, detangling himself from the group hug. "It's getting late,

Let's go check on Mark and get the cars," he decided.

"Good point. We'll get the cars first and leave them at my house," Maddie suggested, eager to search for her husband. "There are too many cars here, and I don't want us to draw undue attention. We should be back in less than an hour."

Less than a day had passed at this point, yet it felt like a month had escaped them. Henry took a seat on the end of the couch, and everyone else followed suit. There, all sat, lost in their own thoughts and staring off into the distance. Eventually, Angie broke the ice by offering to prepare a fresh pot of coffee.

"I will get it," Henry declared with an air of confidence. Angie couldn't help but notice how comfortable Henry seemed in the kitchen, as he moved around with ease.

"It's almost like you're the owner of this place," Angie teased, her eyebrows raised a degree. When did Henry become such an adult?

"Legally speaking, it belongs to me. Cassie left behind all sorts of paperwork, the house title, her poem and various instructions. And, now I'm the new owner!" Henry bragged. Angie chuckled at his boyish charm resurfacing.

"And," Henry continued. "One document she left behind granted me, and two others, legal rights and ownership of the house. Obviously, in the event of her, her husband and her children's disappearances. Although I'm uncertain of the enforceability of said document," he frowned.

"She also stashed away an envelope containing passwords, PINs for her credit cards and an ATM card."

Angie nodded knowingly. "When Cassie and Jules were raptured, I saved their purses, billfolds and wedding rings. I have these in my bag. Speaking of, tomorrow, we should head to the store to purchase the items we will need."

Henry paced the kitchen anxiously, describing the crazy things he'd seen during his hours-long walk home. "I don't want you girls going out alone," he moaned. "It's just not safe! If we travel in pairs, we can gather more groceries, and make the trip more efficient. They have imposed restrictions on everything."

The two gulped down their coffees and walked back to the living room.

In an effort to bridge the group together, Angie asked how each member knew Cassie. Henry, the new homeowner, offered to take the lead on introductions.

"My name is Henry, but people call me 'Pastor,' although I'm not actually a pastor,"

Henry grinned at the others. "Cassie is my aunt, and she took me under her wing. Cassie was a motherly figure to me," he recalled softly.

"And I'll come clean now. For most of my life, I pretended to be a Christian to manipulate my family into giving me what I wanted. I didn't have any genuine interest in building a relationship with Christ. I have been to every Christian rehab facility that would accept me, repeatedly. I've heard the Word. I believed. Yet I knew that if I made Him Lord, I would have to surrender to him. I didn't feel ready to do that. I told Him that at some point, I would commit. Unfortunately, that point never came to pass."

The group fell quiet for a moment as all reflected on Henry's story. Though not in a drug-use sense, his admission resonated with all lost souls in the room. Then, John stood to speak.

"My name is John. Unlike Henry, I won't sound like I'm confessing at an AA meeting," John joked, easing the tension. A few laughed, Henry the hardest. "Like many others, Cassie witnessed to me for a long time. This fell on deaf ears. In short, I believed Christ was a prophet, so I never truly accepted Him. And now, I'm here."

John quickly bowed and reclaimed his seat. His dry sense of humor was similar to Cassie's, Angie noted with a smile.

"Well, everyone is already familiar with myself, my husband Alex, Maddie and her husband Mark, so we can skip these introductions," Angie decided.

"And Rick will be back shortly, if anyone has not yet met him. Jules was his wife; she is his wife; you know what I mean," she continued. Then, she frowned. "I must say, I am curious about Mark. I expected Maddie would have called by now, but I've heard no word."

A short brunette, eyes wet with tears, stood up from a beige sleeper sofa across the room. "Hi," she waved to the group. "This is Davis, my husband," she motioned toward a much taller brunette to her left. "And I'm Lexi. We have three children. They are gone!" Lexi cried uncontrollably.

Davis stood, wrapping his arms tightly around his wife. His expression, too, was pained.

"Our connection with Cassie and her family comes from work," Davis explained, seating his wife back down. "Despite feeling devastated today, we have hope that we will see our children soon. And we're so grateful that they will not have to suffer in the coming years. We will get to know each other's stories more intimately as we spend time together, so that's all for now," he said, and rejoined his wife. He pulled her into another hug.

A man on the adjacent end of the wide living room sniffed a few times, and then rose.

"I am Tyler. I know Cassie and her family from church. I feel like Davis. This is too hard right now. I will just come to know you all in time. I'm actually in awe that we are all here together," Tyler said, locking eyes with each person.

"She spoke all the time about this being her ministry. Cassie was so torn between business and ministry. It took her dear friend, Martha, to convince her that her business was also her mission field," he recalled. "She had such a heart to help people, and her book and the message were so important to her. Her goal was to go around, speak and reach hearts. She just wanted to spread her book and pamphlet to as many people as possible, so they could prepare their family and friends with the message."

"What was the message?" Davis asked.

"I must say, I'm surprised you aren't familiar with this," Henry said, his eyebrows raised. "While churches focused on salvation pre-rapture, Cassie wondered about the fate of her family and loved ones after the rapture. Her mission was to educate people about the mark of the beast and how to avoid it."

"And now that the rapture has commenced, people will soon need a chip, or mark, to buy and sell. Accepting this mark is accepting the Antichrist as your savior, which annihilates any chance you may have of making it to Heaven," Henry emphasized.

"I hear you," Davis responded slowly, the mechanics of his mind whirring away. "So. We can still make things right?" he asked, his voice boldening with determination.

"Yes," Henry agreed. "We have to accept Christ and not take the mark. It will be a tremendous struggle, but since we made our bed, we have to lie in it and make the most of it."

Suddenly, phones around the entirety of the room began wailing. The beeping noise was obnoxious and incessant, echoing off the walls. Moments later, and without warning, a live video began playing on each phone. Even Cassie and Jules' two phones, which had been shut off, sprang to life from the coffee table and began playing the same video.

"It has been exactly twelve hours since the abduction of many of our loved ones around the world," the same cold, robotic female voice from the prior voicemail began. The faces in the room all silently gaped.

"And we are still searching for answers. Those who are missing, according to our investigation, are all individuals who identified with the Christian faith."

The video continued on throughout the next few minutes. It asserted Christianity was the cause for the "major upheaval" in the world, because the group "propagated the belief that those who refused to believe in their Messiah would suffer eternal consequences." This elicited worried yet unsurprised sighs from the members in the room.

"We must come together and unite to ensure a stronger and safer world with these people removed from our path. Our focus is on creating programs that foster unity and aid those who are struggling," the robotic, lifeless woman continued.

"It is necessary that you acknowledge you have heard each nationally issued message, right after it is published. This way, we can ensure that everyone who remains has access to a cell phone. Please notify your friends and family members who don't have one. Should you come across a misplaced phone, do the right thing and give it to someone who could use it. You also may return it to a cell phone store for a hundred-dollar reward."

"The phones will be distributed to those who need them. If you happen upon a phone and give it to someone, request that they visit a local cell phone store to have it transferred to their name. They will receive a six-month waiver on monthly fees so they can communicate with their loved ones during this transition."

The video ended abruptly, and a text message notification immediately appeared on the screen.

The text gave two options. "I have received information regarding the latest update. Please respond with 'yes,' to confirm that you have heard the message, or proceed with listening again to the message."

"Let's hold off on responding," Henry suggested, curious to see what would happen. "According to Tyler, we can't make a phone call without watching and responding to the video first. But I don't have anyone to call," he reasoned, laying his phone down.

"And I'm curious to see how long this will last." Pastor continued.

Lexi nodded quickly, her own plan in mind. "Maddie, can you grab Cassie and Jules' phones? We should reply to their messages and see what kind of response we get."

Maddie agreed and handed one of the phones to Lexi. She held onto the other. The two women huddled around one phone, listening intently to the message. When prompted, Maddie pressed "yes," and the screen lit up with a new text.

"Your phone is linked to a person who has been reported missing. Please provide us with the name and address of the current phone owner," the screen demanded. Maddie input Cassie's address and nervously entered a false name.

Ding! Another message arrived, requesting that she confirm her identity using her primary phone number.

"Does someone know the phone number of her husband?" Maddie croaked, frightened.

Henry's voice caught in his throat as he called out the number for Maddie to type in. Ding! "Your phone number has not been registered in our system."

"They have outsmarted us!" Pastor yelled, now frantic. "I am going to look for Gary's phone. Where is his phone?" He paced the room, ushering people out of their seats and upturning couch and chair cushions. He eventually sat back down, with his head hung between his hands in the image of defeat.

"Gary's phone should be here, unless he wasn't home when he was raptured," Pastor fretted softly. He suddenly stood back up and bolted out of the room.

After a long search, Pastor finally returned, Gary's phone in his hand. He'd found it in the garage, he said. He plugged it in, and instantaneously, or perhaps right before he pushed the cord in, the screen came to life.

Ding!

"The message that came in earlier still requires a response," Pastor told the group, clutching the phone tightly. He clicked on the message, his eyes darting back and forth as he input Gary's name and address.

Ding! His response had been successfully recorded.

The sound of another ding signaled the start of the video. Pastor listened to it once more. Then, the phone flickered and returned to the home screen. "We have Gary registered; now let's check Cassie's phone," he said.

As the man touched Cassie's old phone, a message appeared. "Oh, wait," he stammered, his face pale. "It says 'Your response has been recorded,' but there was more to the message."

"'In what capacity are you related to the owner of this phone?'" he quoted, thumbing the word "husband" and hitting send. His fingers hovered over the keyboard in anxious anticipation.

Ding. "Please submit the last four digits of your social security number to confirm your identity," the message read. Outright frustrated, Pastor swatted the air with his hand and huffed, "I don't know his social security number; actually, I barely know mine."

"If you cannot confirm your identity, it is mandatory that you hand the phone over to a local phone store," the phone responded, as if it were a living creature; breathing, watching, listening. It seemed the government had moved quickly under the guise of this system to "identify missing people."

Their phones were clearly being tracked and monitored, and those without devices would soon have them forced upon them.

Dismayed, Pastor turned to face the group. He vocalized that within the next few days, there would be a record of everyone's location and place of residence.

"Perhaps we should have ignored the first message," Davis frowned regretfully.

Tyler shook his head and reminded Davis that without responding to the initial messages, they wouldn't even have access to their phones, to which Angie sighed in agreement.

"When we use our phones, we trade our privacy for the ability to stay connected and informed," she started. "This started being implemented in March of 2020, when the pandemic hit our country. And that was just the beginning."

"This has been a long-term project in progress," Pastor added.

The door swung open, and in walked Alex and Rick, their heavy footsteps echoing throughout the entryway and living room. Yet Maddie and her husband were still absent, Angie identified immediately.

"Did Maddie go back to her own house for the night, and have you found Mark yet?" Angie asked, as her heart plummeted to her stomach.

"No, Mark was not there," Alex explained. "And Maddie walked in to find her dog, Puddles, pacing the front hallway. Maddie brought Puddles along, but we needed to check if it was okay to bring her into the house. Is anyone here allergic to animals?"

Alex eyed the group, and each member shook their heads, welcoming Puddles to join them.

"Okay, I'll go to the car in a bit and inform Maddie. It seemed like she needed a few moments to herself. Poor girl is experiencing a rollercoaster of emotions. She knew Mark wouldn't be there, but she kept an ounce of hope alive inside that he might still be here," he empathized. It had been a brutal several hours for Maddie, as much as she'd tried to keep her composure.

Alex walked over and embraced Angie warmly, reminding her of how happy he was to see her. "Maddie tells me you are a borderline believer. How did this happen?" he asked, breaking the hug and gazing into his wife's eyes.

Angie laughed wryly as she reflected on the road trip and short stint in Dallas. All of Cassie's words that she'd once mocked had come into fruition, and half of her friend group, and the world, moreover, had vanished. She'd been left behind. Late as it was, who wouldn't believe, at this point?

"Well, listening to Cassie for five hours was exhausting, but it was worth it. Now, the evidence speaks for itself. God used to be an electric fence to me, something to be avoided at all costs. Now, I've jumped the fence, and I'm raring to go," she admitted softly.

"Despite my best efforts to drown out her conversations with music and earphones, I was interested in what she had to say. I was looking forward to having more one-on-one time with her during our trip so we could talk more. I had been seeking answers, but my pride got the best of me. It was tough to admit that the answer to life I'd been aching to find could be so basic; something

I'd heard so many times." Angie sniffed, knowing she couldn't waste time on regrets. She knew the Lord now, and her eternity was hinged upon accepting Him.

"Maddie, what about you?" Davis piped up. "What's your story?"

All faces turned toward Maddie, who had approached the room at some point. She stood in the doorway silently, her old pomeranian sitting beside her. Now that she'd been spotted, she dabbed a tear from her eyes with her sleeve and took a seat beside Angie.

"My upbringing felt like I was immersed in a hypocritical cult. My parents constantly preached about Hell, instilling inside of me a fear of control," Maddie confessed, her tone strikingly sincere.

"And I reached a point where I thought, 'What's the point? No one can make it to Heaven.' So I lived a self-centered life that had nothing to do with Jesus. We all come from different walks of life, but it's clear now that we were all running from Him. Now, it seems we'll be running towards him." Maddie contemplated, her eyes now flickering around the room, absorbing Cassie's impact.

She considered how proud Cassie must feel, right now, watching the impact of her life's ministry from Heaven. And Jules, too, who must have accepted Christ just at the right time. Her heart ached tremendously for her husband and family, but these thoughts gave her a bit of solace.

"I agree," Lexi said with a small nod.

"Well, it's getting late, I know we're all exhausted. Does anyone want to drive home, or should we all just crash here?" Maddie asked. She felt utterly depleted of energy.

John sighed, "I don't want to drive across town. I am like Henry; I live in an apartment, and I don't feel safe. Besides, it feels peaceful here."

Pastor laughed. "Well, now, I just may have a new roommate, if you're on board, John. Although I don't just fear being there by myself; I also prefer being around you guys. With everything considered, you all feel like family. Besides, I don't think any of us should drive in the middle of the night. Nothing is safe anymore."

Angie glanced at Maddie, who sat beside her. Puddles panted on her friend's lap. "Still no word from your husband?" she asked hesitantly.

"No. Not at the house, and no calls," Maddie said shortly. "And if he were somewhere else, he would have called me. I will make peace with the fact that he is gone." Angie nodded sadly, and she reached over and squeezed Maddie's hand a few times.

"We can split up the four rooms," Pastor declared, rubbing his eyes. "Lexi and Davis, you take the guest room; Angie and Alex, you take Cassie and Gary's room. Rick, you can take the twin bed. Maddie, take Kate's room. It was warm and cozy, with a soft rug and a comfortable armchair. John and I can make do with the couches for now."

Then, he snorted in laughter, reminding Angie and Alex that his cousin's room was still his. "But you two can borrow it," he bowed generously, flashing a boyish grin at the married couple.

Maddie gestured for the group to stay put for a moment. "I'm not the best at this," she admitted humbly, "but I think it's important for us to say a prayer before we go to bed."

They all huddled around and held hands while Maddie led them in prayer. After saying "Amen," they hugged each other and said goodnight. The room filled with chatter as couples and individuals gradually dispersed.

"Let's read a bit more before we go to sleep," Maddie suggested to Angie. Angie nodded, grabbed Cassie's computer and headed to the kitchen. Maddie joined her at the table, carrying a steaming cup of tea and a bag of chips.

"Next up is the Day of the Lord," Angie stated matter-of-factly.

Let's go to the Word: The Day of the Lord.

Matthew 24:29 *Immediately after the tribulation of those days shall the sun be darkened, and the moon shall not give her light, and the stars shall fall from heaven, and the powers of the heavens shall be shaken:*

And in Joel 2:30-31 *And I will shew wonders in the heavens and the earth, blood, and fire, and pillars of smoke. The sun shall be turned into darkness, and the moon into blood, before the great and terrible day of the LORD come.*

Do you ever wonder, "Am I righteous in Christ, or am I living a righteous life?" You can study this in depth, #23. The Righteous in Christ and the 5 Crowns awarded in Heaven.

CHAPTER 15

DAWN OF A NEW DAY

THE GRANDFATHER CLOCK STRUCK midnight, chiming gently twelve times. On the eleventh chime, Alex stumbled into the kitchen, disoriented and rubbing his eyes. He wondered aloud if Angie was almost finished.

"Hi love, we're wrapping up right now," Angie assured him. She turned to Maddie and said, "We have not led righteous lives, but we will going forward."

The two women exchanged goodnight wishes, and Angie and Alex left the room. Now alone, Maddie continued to sit, the laptop screen illuminating her face as her mind ventured far away. She recalled her husband and how much she wished he were here with her.

She closed her eyes and listened to the house. She was struck by the stillness that seemed to permeate every room. This juxtaposed the chaos and struggles which awaited the world; these would soon shatter the illusion of security they all felt. Yet even before the rapture, the world had been falling.

We all just ignored the news, the signs and the warnings, and continued on with our frivolous daily lives. We chose oblivion and blindness, she thought. *And now, this was no longer an option.*

Yet occasionally, they had tuned in to the world. Maddie recalled the endless days they spent watching news coverage of the Harvey flood of 2017. She'd felt as though time had come to a standstill. Now, she experienced that same feeling, but tenfold. This was excruciating; time, and all other indicators of "normalcy," had vanished completely.

Finally, Maddie rose, shaking her head abruptly to end her trance. She looked the kitchen over to ensure its tidiness. She placed her tea mug in the sink, shut off the lights and double-checked that the doors were locked. Then, she retired to bed with Cassie's computer.

Maddie planned to spend the night binge-reading about Jesus. When she uncovered the bed, the sight of little Kate's Bible, nestled next to her beloved teddy bear, brought a bittersweet smile to her face. Her tears flowed relentlessly as she cuddled the Bible and bear close to her heart.

Clutching the bear gave Maddie a rush of emotions. She felt loved and safe, as if she had found a companion with whom she could share her deepest secrets. "Kate is gone; it's just you and me, buddy," she whispered to the bear. "I miss her. Do you miss her too? And Cassie. I miss her as well."

Deep down, Maddie knew that the tattered bear was not the right entity to confide in. Still, she found comfort in clutching onto the Bible and talking to the bear. With the teddy snuggled under one arm and the Bible resting on her lap, she leaned back and propped open the laptop. After a quick scan of the next few pages, Maddie realized she wasn't in the mood for a lengthy computer read.

I think I'll read some passages from the Bible, instead, and save these titles for another time, she thought to herself.

"I will put it online as '#24 Significance of the Mount of Olives,' describing the significant similarities and differences in the three dominant religions," she thought.

"And I'll include online, in Cassie's study guide, '#25 Differences in Gog and Magog,' involving the battle of Armageddon and Islamic eschatology."

Maddie's eyes drooped as she read, the stagnant silence broken only by the ticking of a child's purple cat clock, which read almost three a.m. The computer notified her of a dying battery, and as she plugged it in, she noticed several colorful sticky notes on the dresser. She read a few, some containing verses, and others with encouraging lines.

A bright neon green one stuck out, which read, "I am a child of God." Simple yet profound. As she repeated these words over and over in her head, she wondered if Jesus could actually hear her.

"I apologize without excuses." Cassie's words of repentance stayed with Maddie. "People usually apologize to God by simply saying, 'God forgive me; I am sorry,'" the woman had once told her. Not Cassie; she had asked for forgiveness for everything, including the sins she may have unknowingly committed.

Reveal to me the things I need to acknowledge and change, Maddie herself now thought to God. She tilted her head up toward the roof as if gazing into Heaven.

I am not asking for forgiveness so I can continue messing up and running to you for forgiveness. I know you are a loving God, and will forgive a million times. But because I love you, I want to accept responsibility and change anything I have done or continue to do. I humbly request forgiveness from you, Lord, as I search within my heart for any wrongdoing.

Tears continued to pool inside and spill over the brims of Maddie's eyes. She thought each thought urgently.

Once finished with her prayer, she reflected upon the sticky note and the reminder. "I am a child of God." She repeated this in her head until eventually she fell asleep.

The next morning, Maddie left her room to find the others already awake, bustling around the kitchen and preparing breakfast. The noisy sounds of the morning news screeched from the television, reaching her ears, but she wasn't in the mood to listen to this. Maddie longed for solitude, yet she sensed someone or something nearby.

Maddie felt like a new human. Her mind, for once, was silent, all traces of anxiety replaced with a warm and comforting sense of peace. She knew that despite it all, everything would be okay. Despite her desire to read more of Cassie's book, she felt a strong pull to spend the morning talking to God and reading the Bible.

She smiled at this sudden yet familiar urge. Cassie had always had a habit of saying good morning to the Holy Spirit, Jesus and Father God upon waking up, the woman recalled.

Once, Cassie had explained to the girls how she would discuss with God three specific things. She would thank Him for His goodness, praise Him for His infinite greatness, and worship Him for His divine holiness.

Maddie made a mental note to revisit the book on the computer when she got the chance to reread the many verses mentioned. At this point, she was absorbed in reading about the rapture and the Second Coming and was eager to learn more.

Let's go the Word:

The Rapture will occur at any time without warning. Jesus stated in Matthew 24:42–44, *"Therefore keep watch because you do not know on what day your Lord will come... So you also must be ready, because the Son of Man will come at an hour when you do not expect him."*

The Second Coming will be easily recognizable because of the many events that will come before it. As soon as the Antichrist shows up, the clock starts ticking on the seven-year countdown. (Revelation 12:13–17; Zechariah 13:7-9), a treaty with Israel (Daniel 9:27), the rebuilding of the Jewish Temple (Matthew 24:15; 2 Thessalonians 2:3–4; Revelation 11:1-2), followed by the plagues, judgments, and persecutions described throughout the book of Revelation.

With excitement bubbling up inside of her, Maddie tore herself away from the laptop and shared this news with the rest of the group. The verses describing the "Rapture" and the "Second Coming" painted two distinct pictures, clarifying that they would be separate events.

"You will almost certainly want to read this online, #26: The difference between the Rapture and the Second Coming," she read.

"Let's go study this in depth, #27: Why the Tribulation is considered Israel's redemption and Daniel and the timing of the Messiah," the second headline read.

CHAPTER 16

GOOD MORNING TO ALL

WOW, MADDIE THOUGHT INCREDULOUSLY. I have learned a lot, and now, I have a better understanding of the current state of the world. These chapters had revealed to her that the rapture had already happened, the second coming was imminent, and there would be immense wrath during this period.

Lost in thought, Maddie pondered for a moment and thought, "Cassie would have wanted this book to be shared with others, and I feel a responsibility to make that happen."

Maddie ventured into the bathroom, quickly scrubbed her hair, face and body in the shower, and threw on a robe that was hanging on a hook. "Is anyone here?" Maddie shouted from the ajar bathroom door, her voice echoing off the walls.

"We are all in here," Angie hollered in response. "The living room!"

"Could you excuse me for a moment? I have to go grab some clothes from Cassie's room," Maddie told Angie, who now stood against the wall of the hallway. Angie nodded understandingly. Both women had abandoned their suitcases at the Dallas hotel, and Maddie hadn't grabbed any clothes when she had gone to search for her husband.

She and Cassie were practically the same size. And despite the strangeness of it all, she now felt a strong sense of spiritual connection to Cassie.

Glancing at the dressing table in the master bathroom, she noticed one of Cassie's beloved cross necklaces and put it on. She closed her eyes and laid her hand over it, and all at once, she felt a surge of emotion which brought tears to her eyes. She suddenly remembered the other cross necklace she had picked up from the diner floor, and then recalled that she had also taken Jules' wedding ring and necklace.

She took the necklace out of her pants pocket and made her way to Rick, who was huddled on a recliner in the living room. "Rick, I have something for you," she said, and placed the wedding ring and necklace in his outstretched palm.

He gently slid the ring onto his pinky finger and clasped the necklace tightly in his fist. Tears streamed down his cheeks, melting all traces of his normal stoicism. His feelings were surreal. "Is this actually happening?" Rick wondered aloud.

Maddie gave the man a kind, empathetic smile, and handed the other necklace from the bedroom to Angie.

"We are almost ready to eat!" Pastor boomed from the kitchen. The sounds of pots, pans and scattering feet clattered from across the house, and Pastor called out to Angie and Lexi, who were still in the living room, "Do you ladies want coffee, or are you in the mood for some orange juice?"

The two women rushed into the kitchen to lend a hand. With all parties busied, the table was quickly set. Pastor commented, "I'm uncertain how long we'll have access to good food, but conserving what we have will help it last."

"Psst, Maddie," Angie whispered, "you need to check out Cassie's bedroom. She has a bookcase filled with books, CDs, movies and more books."

Angie continued, "On her desk are notebooks filled with pages of research, notes and scribbles that seem to have been made before writing the book."

Maddie's eyes lit up. "We'll discuss everything over breakfast and make a plan of action," she whispered back.

Everyone gathered around the table and eagerly began to dig in, filling their plates and coffee mugs alike. Clearing her throat, Maddie interrupted a few faces mid-bite, suggesting they first say a prayer of gratitude.

"Tyler said we keep forgetting to pray!" she reminded the newly formed family.

"I will pray," Pastor jumped to offer. As the new owner of the household, he was eager to head the group in any way he could. He offered a short yet touching prayer of thanks and protection.

"Wow, Henry! They named you Pastor for a reason," Lexi smiled. "Actually, speaking of, why do they call you pastor?"

The man's eyes flickered down for a moment, traces of shame and loss evident on his face. "Well, I know the Bible," he started slowly. "I once believed it was my calling, but my life took a different course. But, there is still time to win souls!" he stated, resolved to change his ways.

Maddie patted her friend's cousin on the shoulder soothingly, and then faced the group. The expression on her face was severe, and the chattering voices quickly fell quiet.

"We've had some casual conversations," Maddie began, unconsciously adopting the air of confidence and leadership that Cassie once possessed. "But now it's time to delve into more serious matters. We're located along the countryside, some distance removed from the city, but we must remember that we are still close to the suburbs."

"And as we know, our phone announcements are wrong; aliens are in no capacity responsible for the disappearance of all Christians," she emphasized.

"Agreed. If Jules left, then salvation is a one-way ticket," Rick stated, softly stroking the ring on his pinky finger.

Maddie nodded. "I could only describe the event that has just occurred as the rapture. My upbringing has given me some understanding, but Pastor over there may offer more." She met eyes with Henry, who seemed eager to once again honor his original calling.

"I've got this," Pastor nodded. He stood up. "You may have heard of Cassie's poem. The notes behind the poem will provide us with some direction. This, combined with insights from the book on her computer and within her notebook, which Angie just found, will help us manage just fine."

Hesitantly, Lexi raised her hand, as if the dining area were a classroom, and a teacher would emerge to call upon her. "I'm curious; does anyone know what will transpire soon?"

"Cassie's computer holds a condensed version of the information we are looking for. If we print enough copies, everyone can have their own to read," Pastor responded, his mind quickly strategizing.

"You've been so quiet. What do you think?" Davis asked John, glancing at the man. John seemed the quiet-dispositioned type, even aside from the given circumstances.

John spoke quickly. "My religious affiliation is Jewish. I don't read the Bible, only the Torah, so I am at a total loss. I'm just going with the flow. Prior to this, I didn't adhere to the law or go to synagogue regularly, except for observing some of the feast days," he revealed.

"This sounds an awful lot like the Christians who only attend church on Easter and Christmas," Tyler remarked with a short laugh. He then inquired how John knew Cassie, to which the man explained that he and Gary had grown up in the same neighborhood.

"I've known Cassie for almost 20 years now," John said.

Maddie moved her mouth to speak, but a sudden buzzing from every phone in the room drowned her voice out. Everyone turned to pick up their phones, where a tall and charming man awaited them on the screen.

The man was strikingly handsome and dressed impeccably. His eyes were deep green and captivating.

"My name is Jasper Grayson," he introduced himself, his smooth voice as mesmerizing as his appearance. "I regret to inform you that your president is missing. But do not fret; we've already appointed you a new one."

"I'm excited to announce that Theo Wyatt, your new president, and I will work closely together. The UN has replaced your president to ensure the smooth operation of all branches of your government. The UN has determined that the term 'United States' will no longer be used to refer to America," Jasper continued hypnotically. "Many countries believe that the United States has stood alone for too long, and now, we must come together in a unified coalition."

"During these trying times, keep yourself up-to-date on the latest worldly affairs by routinely watching your local news. Our team is working tirelessly to bring together all global leaders to proactively address and combat potential issues. Theo Wyatt is scheduled to give a national address. And I," Jasper said, flashing a glistening smile, "am deeply honored to be chosen as the UN representative replacement, and am committed to doing my best. Together, we will anticipate and proactively address any potential issues."

"Be well," Jasper said, smiling once more. Then, he turned and walked back inside of a large and unfamiliar building.

Several jaws audibly dropped. Otherwise, the silence in the room was deafening.

Minutes later, John finally broke the silence. He pointed out the startling fact that within a single twenty-four hours, their country had lost its president and had already found a replacement. There had been zero mention of neither the Vice President nor the Speaker of the House.

"Theo Wyatt is our new president? I don't know who this is, and he was appointed without a single vote. And who is this Jasper Grayson, that UN representative, who thinks he can just waltz in and change the name of our great country with his smooth talk? After he erases our nation, he tells us to 'be well?'" John gawked, incredulous. "This is unbelievable."

Alex jumped out of his seat, his fists balled. "This situation is unfolding rapidly, faster than the drive-through at a Chick-fil-A!" he spewed. "They have a successor to the throne already, and we haven't even had time to shower."

He continued to vent, yet he knew, deep down, that his words wouldn't change anything. The world was spiraling out of control. They had all known this was coming.

The room was apprehensive to hear what reporters would say about the current situation. Lexi flicked on the remote, and the television sprung to life. The uneasy voices of reporters and screeches from citizens, who ran and lunged around the streets of the capital city behind them, flooded the room.

So this was the outside world.

"Do you all mind if we finish breakfast first, and then continue our talk?" Maddie asked. Breakfast was supposed to be a quick affair, but an hours-long conversation was sparked by the endless list of questions that haunted everyone's thoughts. This conversation continued throughout the evening.

"The next seven years will be a struggle, but eventually, it will end. The first half will be challenging; it will seem like a time of prosperity, amidst the pouring out of what is known as 'wrath.'" Maddie warned. Angie, from across the kitchen, nodded in agreement.

"Cassie stressed the importance of avoiding the 'mark of the beast,' cautioning that this could be a mandatory chip required for buying and selling," she continued.

"I know they've been using chips for years," Lexi interjected with a gasp. "But this sounds like a game-changer! Is it possible that the chips currently in use are a trial version?" The woman cracked her knuckles anxiously.

"The past year has felt like a dress rehearsal. It seems to me that we have been following blindly, like a herd of sheep." Lexi said. Maddie and Angie exchanged glances; her remark was strikingly similar to the car conversations during the four girls' road trip to Dallas.

"Most likely," Maddie agreed. She inhaled deeply, and then continued. "The mark will be mandatory, and those who don't comply will be killed; it's that simple."

"I refuse to be killed," Rick professed adamantly. "I'll take the chip to survive. We need to make sure that someone can buy the food and keep the lights on!"

Angie scowled, her brows turning downward. "Absolutely not. By accepting the mark, you are aligning yourself with the Antichrist!" she declared assertively. Then, her gaze softened some. "Jules, who chose to accept Jesus as her Savior, is now in Heaven," she consoled him.

She knew that somewhere from above, Jules must be watching this exchange. She would not allow her beloved friend's husband to be damned, if she could prevent it.

"Oh," Rick said shyly. He looked extremely overwhelmed. "I'm in," he cleared his throat, trying to sound confident.

"Speaking seriously," Maddie interrupted, "Pastor warned that there may be moments in life when death feels like the better option. The last half of the seven-year tribulation will be so terrible that death and martyrdom may very well seem like the better option. As long as we have accepted Christ, we have nothing to fear."

"And with that, it's getting late," she reminded the group. "We can't afford to waste any more time. Let's pair up and head to the grocery store before it gets dark."

Davis paced the room anxiously. He reminded everyone to fill up their gas tanks first and requested that a detailed grocery list be made. This list should be complete, with a contingency plan, in a pairing needed to purchase more food than originally anticipated, he urged.

To prepare for the household discussion later that night, Angie and Maddie printed out pages from Cassie's books for reference. Maddie wanted to review with everybody a specific, new topic.

Lexi emerged from around a corner, interrupting them. "Do we have plans to stay overnight again?" she asked. "I would like to, but I'm just wondering."

Trumpets, Feast of Trumpets and the last trump. "You can study this online and flip to #28."

CHAPTER 17

NOW I LAY ME DOWN TO SLEEP

FINALLY, IN THE LATE of night, the last pairing made it back to the house. All were utterly drained after an excruciatingly tedious grocery store trip. They'd visited three different stores before they finally found one that allowed standing in line, but the wait was still almost two hours.

The atmosphere had been tense. Police officers were stationed every ten feet. There was a zero-tolerance policy for troublemakers or instigators; they were immediately escorted out of line and sent to their cars. On the first night, following the "disappearances," the lines of people were chaotic and impossible to manage. The intensity of the fights was too much for the police to handle, and looters took advantage of the situation.

Since then, police seized control of the entrances of grocery stores, and they had boarded every window up. Lines now consisted only of people who were grateful for the opportunity to purchase groceries. Each pairing had stocked up on all essentials so the household wouldn't run out of anything they needed.

A full week would pass before they could return to stores. Upon reaching the checkout, shoppers were instructed to download an app and scan it before making their purchase. The system allowed for the accumulation of points with each purchase, but its primary purpose, supposedly, was to limit shopping and prevent abuse.

The explanation made perfect sense given the world's desperate circumstances, but given the earlier conversations of the "chip" and the "mark of the beast," it made everyone feel apprehensive.

The group put away the groceries and cooked a small meal before turning on the television to check on the outside world.

As Alex turned on the TV, they all gathered around the living room. A few fetched extra chairs from the dining room to make room for everyone. The news seemed to occupy every channel, and the images it displayed were more vivid and shocking than they could have fathomed. Smoke filled the air as flames devoured entire buildings, leaving areas of downtown charred and desolate.

The fires, presumably arson-created, left a trail of destruction in their wake as they jumped from rooftop to rooftop. Every inch they touched was obliterated to ash. Fire trucks could not reach buildings because of mass scale wrecks, which had caused roadblocks. Amidst the chaos, groups of firemen frantically wielded hoses and struggled to reach the burning buildings on foot.

The news reported on ongoing fights and blatant shootings, as well as now rampant home burglaries. The internet was abuzz with drone videos capturing unimaginable scenes across different parts of the country. With banks closed and ATMs turned off, it was difficult to get cash. The news advised people to refrain from carrying cash, and instead use credit cards, as a "safer option."

This tracked. The risk of robbery had prompted stores to disallow cash transactions to "minimize the danger to their staff and customers," the party had learned earlier.

"Excuse me," Tyler chimed in, "but isn't the risk the same with credit cards? Credit cards allow for a significantly higher spending limit than just a few bucks in your pocket."

Rick snorted dryly. "It's an escalated continuation of what we saw during COVID. We were explicitly instructed to avoid using cash. Because cash was 'dirty and carried germs,'" he quoted the propaganda from back then. "This contributed to the change shortage, which led to stores only accepting credit cards."

"The convenience of using apps and credit cards has conditioned most people to the idea of a cashless society. This paved the way for the thoughtless acceptance of the chip. If we mold and steer people enough, they won't question the chip; it will seem completely logical."

"And by utilizing an incentive, such as government funding, the chip could encourage more participation!" Rick stood, bordering on shouting. His tone grew more passionate with each passing syllable. "Even before the corona flu hit, America was teetering on the edge of bankruptcy. The amount of national debt we've accumulated since is staggering. I don't see how this country can sustain a higher level of government funding."

"No way," Maddie and Pastor agreed in unison. They shook their heads with rigor. "The funding won't last long," Pastor explained. "Soon, it won't be coming from America. My thought is, our debt is so high that it will be forgiven entirely, if we agree to a one-world government and one-world monetary system. The plan has already been set in motion, and we have been hearing about it for years."

"Do you think the people we'd labeled 'fanatics' were discussing end times so frequently because they saw all these things coming together? That they actually recognized each stage for what it was?" John asked, astonished.

"Precisely," Maddie affirmed, just as Pastor began speaking.

"At some point, we'll need to hide," Pastor interrupted once more. "It's clear that our phones are currently functioning as tracking devices. Registration required us to provide our names and addresses. Soon, we might need to abandon our phones altogether, or have conversations far away from them."

Eyes flickered nervously toward the phones around the room, some on couch cushions or on tables. Others palmed their pockets fearfully.

"You are right," Alex said quietly. "They are rewarding us, if we turn in a phone."

"Ah, I see now," Lexi remarked, as if something had clicked within her. "Sometimes, it feels like our phones have a life of their own. They'll turn themselves on when it's time to send a message, play videos without warning and nag us until we listen. We must acknowledge having heard these messages, or our phone usage will be frozen."

Pastor warned that these obstacles were pale in comparison to events that would soon come.

"As the prophecy states, the Antichrist will rise and a False Prophet will emerge. He will perform miracles that will trick people into worshiping the Antichrist as the Messiah, instead of Christ. If Jasper Grayson is the one, which he might be," Pastor said, recalling the man's striking looks and charm, "They will finally make a peace treaty with Israel. The temple will be rebuilt and the Middle East will finally know peace."

"Is this happening soon?" John inquired.

"Bible prophecy foretells that the Antichrist will erect an idol, in his own likeness, inside the rebuilt temple. The event will take place precisely three-and-a-half years after the peace treaty is signed. That starts the countdown."

Angie nodded. "Inform him about the 144,000 and the two witnesses!" she probed.

Pastor exhaled through his nose. "Cassie left behind so much that it would take several weeks to comb through and study everything. God will mark twelve thousand Jews from each of the twelve tribes of Israel, enabling them to spread their message among their people. People all over the world will accept Christ. Still, countless around the world won't."

"Enoch or Moses will be one of the two witnesses. The other will certainly be Elijah," he continued.

"We've all been eagerly anticipating His arrival," John said. His voice shook with anticipation. "During Passover, it's a tradition to open the door and check if Elijah has come."

Pastor nodded. "As we've discussed, a one-world government, one-world religion and one-world monetary system are underway. By the end of the first three-and-a-half years, many things will have happened. Following Armageddon, Jesus will return for the second time, and a millennium of peace and prosperity will ensue. In short, that encapsulates seven years," he finished.

The air filled with a cacophony of voices. Everyone began speaking at once, each eager to ask their questions.

"The road ahead may be long, but we must stay united. Are there any individuals here who are struggling, and need to take a break, or would like to opt out? Like when Jesus asked his disciples if they were coming or going," Pastor described, his tone serious.

All of his boyish charisma was long gone. Henry now resembled a man; a pastor; a leader.

"*'Then Simon Peter answered him, Lord, to whom shall we go? You have the words of eternal life,'* John 6:68," he quoted.

In unison, they all said, "If not towards Christ Jesus, where else do we go?" Pastor rose and roared, "We are truly the Revelation Generation!"

"Have we identified the Antichrist yet?" Alex inquired, after the room's spirited energy quieted back down.

"Jasper Grayson," Angie predicted. "I think it could be him. I believe he introduced himself without actually introducing himself."

Maddie turned to John and mentioned that she remembered reading a section about Israel's restoration.

"You can go read it online, #29." The Restoration of Israel and Jerusalem.

CHAPTER 18

JUST THE BEGINNING

PASTOR ENTERED THE ROOM with a stack of envelopes. He placed them in the palms of several members of the group. "Not everyone has a letter, but Cassie didn't know everyone would be here. I read mine, and you may want to read it when you have some alone time," he explained.

It seemed that Cassie's preplanning was unprecedented. She had included incredible detailing in her penned letters to family and friends.

The woman had left behind an elaborate letter for her cousin-in-law, in which she'd specified the locations of hidden things that he would need. This included spare credit cards that she had added her nephew's name to. She'd also left spare keys to the cars, a secret storage of cash and other miscellaneous items that she'd hoped they would find useful.

In her letter, Cassie even instructed Henry to use her debit card to purchase necessary items, and empty out her bank account first. Upon reading this, Henry had wondered how long that account would remain active, once she was listed as abducted.

"Where did you find all this?" Maddie asked. Pastor explained that the first letter was in the Bible.

"It was our grandmother's Bible, and I am sure she knew I would pick it up soon. The rest of the messages were retrieved from this wish box," Pastor elucidated, illustrating with his hands the motion of how one might open a box.

"I lifted the lid, and behold, this paper was on top. It said, 'I wish you were here, but I know you will find your way.' But that wasn't all; underneath the Bible was a notebook. Cassie had started a second book, and it looks to be nearly finished! My guess is, her first book had to be published before this one. The second would have been called 'Diaries of a Raptured Woman.'"

Maddie's eyes brimmed with tears. "Cassie believed in a mission that I want to continue," she confided in the group. "Without her, we'd be blind as bats."

"What if Cassie had finished her book before we were all left behind? She would have been able to communicate these vital pieces of information that are rarely discussed. People could have been reminded to warn their family and friends not to take the mark," Maddie grieved.

"None of this was a secret; it is all in the Bible," Angie pointed out.

"Yes, you are right, but most people preach salvation. What if more people had preached what to do if you're left behind?" Maddie explained, growing impassioned. "Cassie taught most of us, and she left us prepared with information in the picture frame at the front door. We all knew to get here and grab this survival guide."

Angie, Lexi, Alex and Pastor simultaneously nodded. Others in the room stood or sat around and listened intently.

"It would be amazing if more people knew about this one little nugget. Look at us; we didn't listen, but we remember that one little seed she planted. And with this, we have a second chance!" Maddie marveled.

"We are now disciples of the post-rapture!" Pastor declared with pride.

Maddie held up a page from the poem that was hanging by the front door. As she gripped it between her fingers, all noticed it was tear-stained, the black ink slightly smudged in some places. The room fell silent in anticipation.

"This is step one," Maddie read. "This page contains the salvation prayer. To receive Jesus as your Savior and Lord, say the following prayer in faith, and He will become your Savior and Lord."

Maddie bowed her head, and the rest of the room followed suit. She read the salvation prayer from Cassie's poem.

"Heavenly Father, I come to You in the Name of Jesus. Your Word says, *'Whosoever shall call on the name of the Lord shall be saved'* in Acts 2:21. I am calling out to you. I pray and ask Jesus to come into my heart and be Lord over my life. Romans 10:9-10: *'If thou shalt confess with thy mouth the Lord Jesus and shalt believe in thine heart that God has raised Him from the dead, thou shalt be saved. For with the heart, man believeth unto righteousness; and with the mouth, confession is made unto salvation.'*"

"I repent, and I ask you to forgive me for all my sins, cleanse my heart, and wash me in your blood. I confess that Jesus is Lord, and I believe in my heart that God raised Him from the dead.

Thank you, Father, that I am now a child of God, and I ask you to guide me, protect me, and set my paths straight so that I will do your will in these last days. In Jesus' name, Amen."

They each whispered the prayer. Tears painted hot lines in their cheeks as they took turns uttering any additional words that came to their hearts. The moment was profound; all were sinners who were left behind, and now they had been redeemed.

They sat together in silence, holding each other tightly as they felt the spirit of the Lord moved through them. Then, one small voice whispered, "Wait."

The speaker was Lexi, who continued, "Not everyone has had the chance to read the poem, the original poem which God gave to Cassie when all this started."

Maddie nodded. "Angie, why don't you share this with everyone?" She suggested.

Angie felt a surge of hope jolt throughout her body. The electricity began within her heart and navigated down her stomach, her legs and feet; up her chest, arms and neck. She stared down at the paper, and after a deep breath, she began to read.

"If you stand before me confused and dazed,

You now see my Words were not in vain.

You have before you this plea I pray,

Heed my words and all I say.

For a second chance just turn the page,

Follow my directions to find your way.

Yes, you will face perilous days,

Fear not, and look upon His face.

Perseverance or a martyr, you will find grace

For in seven years, we win this race.

It will feel like Hell but it's not too late,

Take my hand and find your place,

We will wait for you at Heaven's gate!"

"This is not the end," Angie smiled as tears tumbled down her face. "It's just the beginning for us."

PERSONAL CLOSING STATEMENT FROM CASSIE, OR STACIE, HERSELF

THANK YOU FOR TAKING the time to read this book. My sincere hope is for every reader to be touched in some way by its message. If you are a non-believer, and remain so after reading this, I urge you to carefully consider the words you've encountered. For those who might have strayed away from their faith, may this book serve as a catalyst to rekindle your heart.

To all of the believers with loved ones who are lost, I encourage you to share the contents of this book with them, enlightening them about what lies ahead. Please teach them how to prepare, and primarily, plead with them not to take the mark of the beast that is mentioned in Revelation. For more scriptures that directly reference this, see the list at the end of this letter.

As you read this text, I pray that you also have the opportunity to turn the spiritual page and make the necessary changes in your life.

If you have loved ones who need to hear this vital message, I invite you to plant the seed of awareness within their hearts. A simple and meaningful way to do this is by gifting them a framed family picture or your own heartfelt poem, or you may use the one provided in this book. Alongside it, leave a letter with detailed instructions for what to do, if they do find themselves left behind.

These are just a few ideas, and the opportunities are boundless. The objective is to support and guide your loved ones through impending troubled times. This includes family, friends, co-workers, or neighbors you have been sharing your beliefs with. Be like Cassie, allowing them access to your home if the rapture occurs.

1. Leave a personal letter for them, sealed in an envelope, perhaps in a "wish box," detailing everything you wish to convey to them.
2. Provide them with essential items such as a copy of this book, a study guide, a Bible, cash, a debit or credit card in their name, spare keys to your car, and instructions for finding anything hidden they may need.

3. Consider creating a will, which may not necessarily grant them legal rights to your property, as Cassie's loved ones understood. We can't anticipate every detail of what lurks ahead, but it is far better than having nothing prepared. They do not need to know about it until the appropriate time arrives.
4. The advantage of simply informing your loved ones about a framed message at your door is that it keeps things simple and direct for those who may not listen intently. You can just say, "In the event of the rapture, please make your way to my house and check behind the frame." If the rapture occurs during their lifetime, they will recall this and head to your home immediately, and you will have helped them prepare.

You can visit our actual website to download the study guide, read our blog or email us for questions. You can even purchase a copy of an artwork from a local artist that was painted to go along with this book. It would be a great picture to hang in your house with instructions placed behind it.

TheRevelationGeneration.com

The primary reference to the "mark of the beast" is found in The Book of Revelation. Here are the verses from the NIV Bible:

Revelation 13:16-18 It also forced all people, great and small, rich and poor, free and slave, to receive a mark on their right hands or on their foreheads, 17. so that they could not buy or sell unless they had the mark, which is the name of the beast or the number of its name. 18. This calls for wisdom: let the person who has insight calculate the number of the beast, for it is the number of a man. That number is 666.

Revelation 14:9-11 A third angel followed them and said in a loud voice: "If anyone worships the beast and its image and receives its mark on their forehead or on their hand, 10. they, too, will drink the wine of God's fury, which has been poured full strength into the cup of his wrath. They will be tormented with burning sulfur in the presence of the holy angels and of the Lamb. 11. And the smoke of their torment will rise for ever and ever. There will be no rest day or night for those who worship the beast and its image, or for anyone who receives the mark of its name."

Revelation 15:2 And I saw what looked like a sea of glass glowing with fire and, standing beside the sea, those who had been victorious over the beast and its image and over the number of its name. They held harps given them by God.

Revelation 16:2 The first angel went and poured out his bowl on the land, and ugly, festering sores broke out on the people who had the mark of the beast and worshiped its image.

Revelation 19:20 But the beast was captured, and with it the false prophet who had performed the signs on its behalf. With these signs he had deluded those who had received the mark of the beast and worshiped its image. The two of them were thrown alive into the fiery lake of burning sulfur.

Revelation 20:4 I saw thrones on which were seated those who had been given authority to judge. And I saw the souls of those who had been beheaded because of their testimony about Jesus and because of the word of God. They had not worshiped the beast or its image and had not received its mark on their foreheads or their hands. They came to life and reigned with Christ a thousand years.

A BRIEF OUTLINE OF THE SEVEN YEARS WHICH FOLLOW THE RAPTURE

WE EACH HOLD VARYING beliefs related to Christ, Heaven and Hell and the concept of the rapture. If these notions find no resonance within your heart, I invite you to consider the perspective these words hold, because your soul is at stake! I will make the claim now that if I am wrong, then I have wasted my time. If you are wrong, you will waste your eternity. If you have family members or friends who do not believe, I implore you to give them a copy of this book. Maybe write them a letter to leave alongside this.

When the rapture happens, millions will leave earth in the blink of an eye. The world will fall to chaos, and those remaining will have a perilous time determining what to do next. If you have heard the Gospel, you are more likely to begin following Jesus after the rapture. If you have never heard of the rapture, you will be at a total loss.

Should your circle encompass those who are yet to embrace these beliefs, a fervent plea arises to extend this knowledge to them. Consider, if you will, sharing this book, accompanied by a heartfelt letter that bears the weight of your affectionate care.

Imagine the scene as millions depart from our realm in an instant, transcending the boundaries of earthly existence. In their wake, a world stands poised on the precipice of tumultuous transformation, struggling to find its bearings amidst the upheaval. Yet, for those familiar with the Bible, there emerges a glimmer of guidance, a glint of hope that draws them toward the path of Jesus.

For those who have yet to acquaint themselves with the concept of the rapture, a bewildering void may envelop their being, leaving them adrift in a sea of uncertainty. The coming days are documented in the Old and New Testament.

The world will be in shambles, with countless desperate souls searching for family members and trying to sort out what has happened. There will be a one-world leader, called the Antichrist, who will seemingly bring order and peace (Revelation 6:1-2). He will sign a peace treaty for

Israel (Daniel 9:27). The third temple in Israel will be rebuilt. This will be the official beginning of the seven-year Tribulation; The Time of the End.

A False Prophet, accompanying the Antichrist, will perform false miracles and promote a one-world religion. He will convince people to worship the Antichrist, or leader (Revelation 13:11). There will be a one-world government, with a single world monetary system, in which the chip, which is the "mark of the beast," or "666," will be mandatory.

The chip will be required to buy and sell, but you will not enter Heaven if you accept it. Taking the mark is accepting and worshiping the Antichrist as your savior, just as Christians accept Christ as our Messiah. Reference Revelation 14:9-11.

To the nonbeliever, "end day" discussions may seem like a mad conspiracy. Yet, worldly elements are already aligning themselves in this direction.

We are already taking strides toward becoming a cashless society, with circulating talk of a "chip" to make purchases and keep track of a person. If you do not take the mark at that time, you will be unable to buy or sell anything. You may be killed, unless you flee and hide. However, despite all earthly consequences, it's critical you do not take it.

It is far better to be martyred than to live through the final seven years on earth.

If you are left behind, accept Christ Jesus as your savior. The span of the "End Day" events following the rapture will last seven years. At the midpoint, three and a half years, the temple will be desecrated by the Antichrist. He will claim he is God.

The second half of the seven years is called the "Wrath of God." You do not want to be living during this time. God will send two witnesses; Elijah is one, and Enoch, or Moses, is the second. They will be killed and will lay in the streets for three and a half days. Then, they will come back to life in front of the eyes of the world, and God will call them back to Heaven.

144,000 Jews will witness these events around the world. There will be seven seals, seven trumpets, seven bowls and seven thunders, or wraths, people will endure.

At the end of the seven years, the Euphrates River in Iraq will run dry. A massive army will cross this land to wage the battle of Armageddon in Israel. If you doubt this, a swift Google Map search will depict the rate at which the Euphrates has begun drying up within the last few years.

Then, Jesus will return with the Saints who were raptured. Just by speaking, Jesus will destroy the armies at Armageddon. The Antichrist and the False Prophet will be cast into Hell. The Bible also states that Satan will be cast into a deep pit for a thousand-year period, and will at some point be released for a short time.

Many other events will conspire in the midst of these turbulent seven years. If the rapture has not yet occurred at the time you read this, I urge you to choose Christ. If you still don't believe, and you find, one day, that millions are missing, know then that Christ is the Messiah and DO NOT take the chip. I reiterate that this is the one unforgivable blasphemy.

Jesus will return at the end of the seven years. He loves you so much that even if you have lived your life rejecting Him, He still will give you a final chance to repent and accept Jesus as Messiah. God sent us His Son. Much of the world has already rejected Him, but if you are left behind, you will know this as truth.

ABOUT THE AUTHOR

STACIE BOWLES IS A Texas-based author and devoted Christian with a passion for evangelism that has defined much of her life's work. Having attended the prestigious Reinhard Bonnke School of Evangelism in 2016, one of her greatest honors, Stacie has dedicated herself to spreading the teachings of Jesus Christ. Guided by the Holy Spirit and the wisdom imparted by various pastors, she believes that her spiritual education stands as her most significant life accomplishment.

Stacie is the author of ***For a Second Chance, Turn the Page,*** a ground-breaking book that addresses the urgency of understanding the prophetic narrative surrounding the end times. Unique in its approach, the book urges Christians to prepare spiritually and educationally for the loved ones who might be left behind. With years of in-depth Bible study to back her, Stacie sees this work as especially timely given her conviction that we are nearing the prophetic age described in the scriptures.

Stacie's life mission transcends traditional boundaries, focused as she is on sharing the redemptive power of Christ's love. With ***For a Second Chance, Turn the Page,*** she hopes not just to inform, but also to equip her readers with the knowledge and inspiration they need to prepare for the uncertain times that lie ahead, ultimately aiming to guide them toward the eternal grace of the Lord.

Aside from her spiritual and literary pursuits, Stacie is deeply family-oriented, valuing quality time with her loved ones above all else. A dedicated self-employed stay-at-home mother, she cherishes simple yet meaningful activities like discussing life and faith over coffee with friends, emphasizing the importance of creating lasting memories, and running her own business.

Made in the USA
Las Vegas, NV
18 April 2024

88821938R00148